CW00538788

LAMDA
SPEAKING MATTERS
A practical guide to speaking in public

Volume 3

First published as *Speaking Matters* in October 2010 and revised in 2015
This edition first published in 2019 by the
London Academy of Music and Dramatic Art (LAMDA)
155 Talgarth Road, London W14 9DA
Tel: +44 (0)208 834 0530
www.lamda.ac.uk

Edited by Vinota Karunasaagarar

Printed by: Hobbs the Printers Ltd, Totton, Hampshire, SO40 3WX
Concept design and layout: Neil Sutton, Cambridge Design Consultants
Illustrations by Neil Sutton
The original diagrams were drawn by Lucy Atkinson

ISBN: 978-0-9932443-4-6

Contents

Foreword

Founded in 1861, LAMDA is the oldest drama school in the UK. We started to offer examinations in speech and drama to the public over 130 years ago. Since then we have developed an enviable reputation for excellence in the provision of Communication and Performance examinations in the UK, and we are rapidly extending our reach internationally.

The process of preparing for and succeeding in a LAMDA Examination helps Learners, whatever their ages or aspirations, to develop a broad range of skills that will serve them throughout life. Our examinations develop a Learner's ability to:

- read easily, fluently and with good understanding
- expand vocabulary to improve powers of self-expression
- improve confidence in speaking and listening
- memorise and recall information
- research and create persuasive formal presentation
- create and defend arguments
- engage in constructive informal conversation
- work both on their own and participate as a member of a team.

No matter what direction Learners choose to follow in the future, our examinations provide the opportunity to nurture their natural abilities. These critical skills will enhance their self-confidence to engage and contribute fully, whether at school, in further education, at work or in the community. In other words, to fulfil their potential.

All our examinations are rooted in encouraging Learners of all ages to develop a love of literature, poetry and drama and thus improve standards of communication through the spoken word.

Ultimately, it is a sense of achievement that empowers the Learner. We believe that succeeding in a LAMDA Examination demonstrates not only that they have met rigorous Assessment Criteria in a particular discipline, but also that they have grown as individuals through participating in a worthwhile activity that is respected as a global standard.

Thanks

LAMDA would like to thank all of the contributors who assisted with this and the previous versions of this book: Clarissa Aykroyd, Faye Carmichael, Jacque Emery, Greg Hamerton, Linda Macrow, Christopher Marlow, Stephen Owen, Norma Redfearn and Christina Williams.

Introduction

Why does speaking matter?

The spoken word has power. The right words at the right time can move minds. You might need to convince the committee, persuade the public, or simply get the job. The better you are at communicating, the better your ideas will seem and the more success you will have in motivating people.

If you are preparing for a speech you need to research, structure and present your material in the best way. This book provides methods that you can learn quickly.

Although many of us have strong skills in conversation, speaking in public requires special techniques that we do not usually employ. Such techniques are invaluable in formal situations, when we need to enhance our speech to reach an audience.

Public speaking holds a special terror for many people. It is natural to be fearful of things you do not know how to do. You probably have a lifetime of conversational skills to draw on. All you need are the tools to transform those skills into powerful advantages. With effective preparation, you can remove the fear, think clearly and develop a great performance. By learning simple techniques, you can add impact to your speech, discover how to persuade people and begin the journey to becoming an effective speaker.

Whether you intend to speak from the stage or lead a group discussion, this book will assist you. Improving your communication through the spoken word will build your confidence and self-esteem, which will help you to succeed.

What this book covers

This book presents the knowledge required to develop your communication skills, from basic speaking skills to the technical aspects of how to prepare and present your speeches in public.

This book includes useful information for LAMDA Examinations and should be used in conjunction with other information books and teaching resources.

You will find examples of great speeches that demonstrate important techniques, definitions of technical terms and exercises to develop your speaking skills in key areas.

Planning and Preparation

Good preparation allows you to become confident and knowledgeable. This improves your ability and leads to more speaking opportunities. It all begins with good planning. In this chapter we will discuss how to select your subject matter and how to adapt your speech to suit your audience, situation and purpose.

Preparation will help to improve the quality of your speech. Examinations assess and encourage progress, but much planning and preparation needs to take place before you are ready to perform well under examination conditions.

How to select your subject matter – choosing a topic

Sometimes you are given a topic to speak about. Ask yourself as many questions as you can about the assignment. What are you expected to present? Is there one area within that topic you should focus on? What kind of speech should it be – a quick discussion, a conversation, or a presentation? The way the assignment is phrased and who it is for can give you important clues.

For example, '**Discuss** dogs and cats with members of the Cat Society' means you are preparing for a conversation in which the easy approach would be to talk about why cats are better than dogs.

'**Present** the sleeping habits of cats and dogs' suggests a speech with some images showing both animals asleep and some interesting facts based on recent studies that people might not know about. Do cats sleep more? Can you wake a dog more easily?

'**Give a speech** on how dogs used to be more useful than cats' suggests you will need to research the history of how dogs were useful in the past (perhaps they protected their owners or livestock from wild animals). You should contrast that with how this has changed. Many people have moved to the cities – perhaps cats are more useful as companions in small living spaces?

'**Tell the story** of your favourite dog' means you can have fun and narrate the dog's life in brief, from beginning to end, sharing the most interesting stories that show its character.

You can interpret topics in many ways. For example, given the topic of 'Are dogs better than cats?' you can decide to investigate their intelligence, or their usefulness, or the cost of keeping them. The question suggests you should debate the topic (points for dogs, points for cats and then declare the winner). In all cases, it is important to keep your speech linked closely to the stated topic – discussing how you once owned a rat would be off-topic unless you are using the rat to demonstrate how your cat and your dog reacted differently to it (one ignored it, the other ate it).

If you are given a few topics to choose from, choose one that you really care about and make it relevant to your audience. This gives you two advantages: it is easier to engage an audience when the speech you are making is useful to them, and when you speak about something you care about, you can be more enthusiastic.

You can use the same approach when selecting your own topic and when trying to refine your given topic. Begin with topics that will be most relevant to your audience. Then find the one that means the most to you, because you can be passionate about it.

Once you have developed some skill in public speaking, you might be asked to select a challenging topic. These are often on **controversial subjects** (moral, ethical or political issues). You have to take great care to offer a balanced speech (presenting both sides of the issue). If you try to offer a resolution or need to state your position, do so near the end of your speech and be sure to respect members of the audience who might hold different views. Be prepared for all situations, including a potentially unreceptive audience. Extra research is required to ensure you understand the latest developments and have a good command of the subject. Always keep your speech relevant to your audience – the points you focus on must have a direct application to the audience members, dealing with real issues that they face. Use important facts that inform them about the current issues with clear logic that supports any statements.

If you are delivering a **motivational** speech, build it around a message that really matters to you – it will be easier to be sincere if you believe that the message will improve your audience's lives. By focusing on the message instead of yourself, you will find greater confidence in your speech.

Researching your topic

STEP 1   Having decided on the subject of your speech, it is time to **collect** information about it. Gather more than you need, because you will be more confident when you are fully informed. You can discard the irrelevant facts as you adapt your speech to suit your audience, situation and purpose.

The internet can be used to collect relevant and interesting information about a particular topic. However, exercise caution with commercial websites, as they could be trying to sell a product and may, therefore, present information in a biased way. Also, be wary of sites full of opinion and commentary (blogs or forums), where the participants could be uninformed and more eager to be read than to be accurate. A good place to start is on a website where the content is compiled either by or for professionals in their field; for example, if you require information about where your nearest general practitioner (GP) is, you could start by looking at the NHS website.

The local **library** is a good research venue, because their books and digital resources often contain high-quality information, and librarians can help you with your research.

For a more current source of information, radio and television programmes can be considered in your research. Other sources of information are newspapers and magazines, although some tend to focus on current events, opinion and politics and supply little information of lasting value. Consider who is presenting you with the information and it will become easier to find useful articles.

Publications which focus on a particular subject, such as history or geography, may be a more reliable source of information than tabloid newspapers or celebrity gossip magazines.

Commercial database sites provide a good collection of newspapers, periodicals and financial information. Again, this may be something that your local librarian can help you with. Collect articles that surprise you with facts you did not know or things your audience would find remarkable.

Conversing with people directly can provide another source of information; for example, by conducting interviews. However, be aware that while this may provide valuable information from a personal or collective point of view, the information provided can also be biased.

STEP 2 When you have collected enough information, **read** and re-read what you have. This allows your mind to build a single picture of the facts you have to hand, which makes the next step easier.

STEP 3 **Sort** the information, removing findings from your research that you think are irrelevant or inappropriate for your speech and to the audience you will be presenting to. Then rank those that remain so you can plan where to include them in your speech.

STEP 4 Based on the facts, **make notes** about your own feelings and conclusions to include in your speech. Be aware of copyright, as you may not be able to quote articles word for word without acknowledging the source.

This process of collecting, reading, sorting and making notes leads to a successful speech. It is easy to prepare a long-winded speech; it takes far longer to prepare a short speech with impact.

In an examination situation, time is of the essence. You need to share your thoughts and ideas clearly and with spontaneity. Prepare according to the syllabus: the Assessment Criteria will guide you to develop essential skills as you progress through the grades.

How to adapt your speech

Having collected information and before you begin writing, you must **consider the audience, the situation and the purpose of the speech**, as these must guide your choice of material and your style of presenting. Consider this early on, so you can adapt your vocabulary and sentence structure to ensure that your speech is relevant and focussed in an individual way that will make it effective.

If you are preparing a speech for a LAMDA Examinations you will find that the syllabus is a useful framework. Check that the work being prepared fulfils the relevant criteria.

Who is your audience?

The nature of your audience will guide many choices in the planning process. Try to be as specific as possible, using the following questions to ensure you know as much about your audience as you can:

- How many people are in the audience?
- What groups of people are in the audience?
  (Consider their age, gender, nationality, faith, occupation, activities and so forth.)
- Do any groups of people have a special interest or specialised knowledge of one subject?

Collect information about the groups of people you have identified. Your host might also provide details of the likely audience.

The venue, date and time of the speech is also useful information, which will determine what type of people could attend. Study publications and websites that these people would read. Meet some of them before the event for casual conversation.

Understanding your audience allows you to select relevant topics and to adapt the language, content and style to make them appropriate. It also helps you to contrast these elements in speeches for different audiences. For example, if you are speaking to **children**, you can expect them to have a short attention span. Create many short variations on the same topic to keep them interested. Reduce the length of arguments to keep things simple and use a plain, logical style.

Base your speech on what your audience knows so they can relate to what you're saying. If you are giving a speech on Artificial Intelligence (AI) for the workplace at a Tech Fair, it is likely that the audience are already interested in this area and have a familiarity with this subject matter, as they have chosen to attend the fair. However, the same speech to a group of office workers, at the request of their employer, may have audience members who are unfamiliar with the subject matter, so the speech will have to be tailored to explain what AI is and how this is relevant to the work they do.

When presenting to a **group** – for example, a faith group – be aware of the group's, views on the topic that your are presenting and treat these views with respect. In this case, depending on what your speech relates to, there may be no need to convince them of your argument, as it could be on a topic that they already agree with, but you could also look at opposing views and explain the need for tolerance and understanding. The advantage of speaking to a group is that your arguments can be based on their beliefs, but treat their viewpoints sensitively.

Since most audiences are made up of both **men and women**, avoid using unnecessary gender-specific language where possible (*'Mankind* has been here for 200,000 years. *He* will be here for a long time still…'). While such expressions may sometimes be necessary, you should avoid language that sounds sexist or makes one gender sound more important than the other.

Understanding the audience is thus a key step to preparing your speech well. A lot can be learned about your audience by thinking of them in a basic, common-sense way. You want to discover the one common factor that unites them so you can adapt your speech accordingly.

Ask yourself 'Who are they?' and 'What do they want?' This allows you to produce a list of key audience points, which will guide the development of your speech. Then, by asking 'What are they worried about?' you will help you to identify the most important issue. If you can present the solution to their problem you will have an attentive and delighted audience.

The mood of the audience

It makes a big difference to your approach if you can guess whether the audience will be friendly, neutral, reluctant, prejudiced, hostile or enthusiastic. A **friendly** audience will be easy to please: they are happy that you have come to discuss the topic, so apart from sharing worthwhile content with them, you can engage them with humour and entertain them with anecdotes.

With a **neutral** audience, you must be enthusiastic about your subject to win them over to your side. Once you have established a link with the neutral audience, you can play with them a little: for instance, by setting up an opposing point of view before knocking it down with your logic or by asking a rhetorical question.

A **reluctant** audience have better things to do than listen to you. Perhaps they are required to attend or they have their own agenda at the meeting. To speak effectively to them, your topic must be very relevant. Every example, quote, anecdote and visual aid must be aptly chosen.

The **prejudiced** audience have already made up their mind on the topic you are presenting. You will have to spend a lot of time establishing common ground, showing that you understand their feelings and that you share their concerns before suggesting any alternative attitude or solution.

With a **hostile** audience, you will have to say things the audience will agree with and build your argument in small steps to bring them to your desired conclusion. Leaps of logic, vague metaphors and humour are unlikely assistants. Present clear, undisputed facts that are linked tightly to the common cause of the audience. If you are going to express an opinion, do so at the very end, when you have demonstrated the infallible logic of your position. Persuade them!

An **enthusiastic** audience can be daunting, but they can also be one of the most engaging and interactive audiences you can present to. Developing a relationship with this type of audience is crucial, as once they are on your side they are a valuable asset and are able to enhance the performance of your speech. Keep this audience from consuming the energy of your speech and distracting away from your topics by involving them in the speech. For example, allow them time to laugh, as this will make pulling the focus back to your topics easier, and maintaining good eye contact can help dictate when there is a switch in tone and can allow you to dictate the pace of your speech. Remind the audience when it is time to be more serious by adjusting your body language, slowing your speaking pace and drawing the energy of the room back to you. Above all, make sure you focus on the purpose of your speech.

What is the purpose of your speech?

Have you ever listened to a speech and asked yourself: 'What on earth was the point of that?' To make an impact on your audience, you must speak with clarity of purpose, producing a speech that makes a point. A clear purpose leads to effective communication.

Carefully consider these guiding questions to develop a well-crafted speech:

1 *What do you want your speech to do?*
   - to **inform** your audience,
   - to **entertain** them,
   - to **challenge** them or
   - to **persuade** them to agree with your viewpoint by challenging their thinking.

2 *What **action** do you want the audience to take because of your speech?*

You can use a combination to give the speech more impact, but first establish your **primary purpose**. You should use it in the title as well: for example, an entertaining speech about rabbits might be *Rabbiting On*. An informative speech would be *The Life Cycle of the Rabbit*. A persuasive appeal would be *Save the Rabbits from the Gun*.

What is the situation?

The *situation* means the setting of your speech: for example, an interview in a busy newspaper office, a meeting at a church or an address to a family at a funeral. The situation could be as simple as a conversation with a friend. Situations can be broadly divided into formal and informal.

Formal situations are official or important occasions where you would be expected to dress smartly, behave politely and use cultured language. There is often a seated audience present, which may be large; for example, a business conference or seminar.

In **informal** situations the audience is usually small, the event is unstructured and a casual appearance is acceptable, such as an afternoon event run by a local community centre or group.

You should plan your speech to fit the situation. Think about the room and decide beforehand where you are going to stand or sit in relation to the audience to make the most of the space (see chapter *Engaging the audience* for more on using the space). Bear in mind that in some situations – for example, a business conference – you may be required to stand behind a fixed lectern because of the sound and lighting arrangements of the organisation and venue.

Plan what you will wear and ensure it matches the style of your speech and the audience it is intended for. Your appearance helps to establish the formality or informality of the situation. Use these elements to your advantage, showing how effective and versatile you can be as a communicator. You can adapt your speech to suit any situation.

Interview: An interview is usually formal, even if you are expected to dress in a casual style. Your appearance is vital here: pay extra attention to your posture, body language and clarity of speech. Every employer prefers good communicators. Having the skills for a job is only half of the challenge – convincing the employer that you are the best requires some dynamic communication. Researching the company would be wise, and extra preparation on subject areas you are likely to be asked about will give you a confident air.

Meeting: Every meeting has an agenda: a reason for bringing the people together. To achieve the purpose of the meeting, your speech must support that agenda, so you need to cut out material that introduces conflicting ideas. Remove facts that might be interesting but involve issues that are off the main topic. Tailor the speech to cause the particular action you wish those attending to take.

Training group: as a presenter in a training group, it is important to ensure that the knowledge you wish the training group to acquire is fully transferred.

You should first try to establish the level of your audience and be prepared to alter your speech, which means you might need to prepare three levels of complexity (basic, intermediate and advanced). If you are contracted to train staff, you should arrange a meeting with the person who booked you (usually this is the Human Resources (HR) department) to ascertain what outcomes are required and the knowledge level of your audience. You can then devise the course accordingly before you attend.

Most training should be interactive and highly practical to be effective. Allow for questions during your speech, even though this may upset your plan with unexpected challenges and diversions. Trim the content of your speech down as you go along to make time for this, and be prepared to do this before you attend – so you come to the training with sections that you can skip if the session overruns.

Address: An address is usually part of formal proceedings, which means you will have a set time for your speech. Practise your speech to ensure that you can always keep to the time limit. Pay more attention to preparing language that is appropriate to the occasion. Develop your projection techniques to ensure your voice will carry your message to a larger audience.

Public engagement: As this is probably a large gathering, if you are able to prepare by scheduling a technical rehearsal with all visual aids at the venue, then you should do so. This will also provide you with the opportunity to practise on the microphone. However, for most public engagements the opportunity to rehearse with sound systems or visual aids is rare. Hence, you should be aware of microphone techniques before using one. Important occasions will usually have a sound engineer on hand who will balance the sound as you speak.

When preparing your speech, be sure to state the issue up front, for media quotes. Extra practice is recommended because this is probably high-pressure presenting, and being in the spotlight can be intimidating. Take extra care to research the audience well, and tailor your speech to establish common ground that you share with the audience before leading them onward.

Live online interview: This can take many forms: audio, text, video or a combination of all three. People may log in and out as the interview continues, so restate your purpose from time to time. Consider the international nature of your audience by using clear and simple language. Short answers are best, especially if the interview is being transcribed.

Matching topics to the audience and selecting your content

Use your research on the audience to guide you. Effective communication involves both the speaker and the listener, so knowing what will appeal to an audience is important. You need to *share* thoughts and ideas, rather than merely transmit information. To achieve that, you need to find **topics** (general subject areas) that the audience will find interesting rather than topics that interest only you. You should gather more information about your chosen topic than you need so that you can select the material that is most relevant and appropriate to your audience, purpose and situation.

The **content** is made up of the specific aspects you choose to include in your speech. Use your knowledge of your audience to match the content to the needs and interests of that particular group. For example, the topic of renewable energy might be a good topic for a group of environmentalists but how to fix a wind-turbine blade might not be appropriate content for them because it is not relevant to their environmental cause. They would be more interested in how effectively a wind-turbine produces power, and whether there are more efficient alternatives.

To find an appropriate topic and the right content, ask questions like:

- What do I want them to know?
- How much do they need to know?
- How much can they absorb?
- What will interest them?
- What can I do to involve them?
- What is the audience expecting?

You may be as specific or as general as you like, but make sure you match the content of your speech to the audience.

You may need to reflect upon your material for some time to allow the main themes to emerge from the information before you. Once you have discovered a clear, logical progression that you intend to follow, select the material which supports that logic. **Evaluate** the material and rank it from weakest to strongest – information that supports the theme or your argument most clearly takes priority. The evaluation of material should not be hurried because your speech will stand or fall on the strength of your chosen information.

Select the best points and then establish a progression by presenting the simplest or weakest first and working your way towards the climax. Complex concepts should come later in the speech. Give your audience time to consider what you are saying. You should aim to empower, not overpower, your listeners.

SPEAKING MATTERS

Using the right language

You already use language to communicate your thoughts, feelings and ideas to other people. It is natural to adapt the words you use to suit the people you are talking to. For example, do you speak to your friends, teachers, grandparents and police officers in exactly the same way? Probably not – you change and modify the way you speak automatically, without having to think about how you do it. You can instinctively judge the degree of formality or informality that guides the way you address people.

Having a clear idea of your audience, the situation and the style of your speech helps you to use the right language. If, for example, you were to prepare a speech on road safety to a group of adults in the same way as you spoke to children in a nursery, then the language would be inappropriate.

Two elements of language you can easily adapt are **vocabulary** and **sentence structure**. Vocabulary means the range of words you use. Simple words are more useful with younger audiences or those unfamiliar with English, and with settings that are informal. A more advanced vocabulary is useful when speaking to highly educated or specialised audiences.

Variety in your language keeps the audience interested. One of the ways this can be improved is by using an extensive vocabulary, so use a dictionary and thesaurus when preparing your speech. You can use descriptive language when sharing feelings, plain language during explanations, and bursts of energetic language in those moments when you want the audience to take special notice of your words.

Sentence structure is a matter of choice. Long sentences with many conjunctions can lead to complications, which you might not have intended, and confusion within your audience about what you mean. Short sentences are simple. They can be more powerful. But too many close together can make you seem abrupt. And short sentences will slow your speech down, because of all the pauses. Again, variety is important, so vary the sentence structure to achieve a flow that supports the message you are trying to convey.

The language you use to communicate with your audience must seem natural and appropriate. If you have adapted your language to match the particular situation, you demonstrate that you are an effective communicator.

If an occasion is formal, then formality and using the **correct** language becomes important. Using a slang phrase – for example, 'I was chuffed' instead of 'I was delighted' – reduces the formality of your language. Saying 'We was delighted' when you mean 'We were delighted' is incorrect grammar. Practise your speech in front of people and invite their reactions, to catch your mistakes.

Be restrained in your use of intensified words. If everything on your trip was 'amazing', the people 'incredible', the views 'spectacular' and the meals 'out of this world', all the descriptions lose their power and your audience will not believe you.

Be aware that the language of speaking is different from the language of writing. Writing allows for longer, complex sentences (because readers can skip back to make sense of things) and more advanced vocabulary. It often sounds stilted and formal when read aloud.

Curse words are inappropriate in almost all settings and although they might have a big effect, it will probably not be the effect you are hoping for. It is likely that you can find a more appropriate word that is more descriptive and thus does a better job of communicating your thoughts.

Technical terms need to be explained clearly unless your audience consists entirely of specialists who are familiar with the terminology.

You can use certain **words for effect**. A thesaurus can be useful here. There are often many similar words which can describe the same thing, but certain words have more power and impact. Such words can be effective, but only if they have associations for your audience. For example, if you are supporting your government, they are a 'tough administration'. If you are criticising them, they may be a 'repressive regime'.

Avoid the temptation to use obscure words, which demonstrate your technical vocabulary, but the audience are unlikely to understand. The same message can often be said with simple, everyday language with more impact.

Timing

Timing is crucial for a successful speech. As part of your preparation, you should be aware of how much time you have been allocated to deliver your speech. If your speech is too short you may not have enough time to engage with your audience and if it's too long you run the risk of your message becoming lost.

Preparation is essential; make sure you rehearse beforehand. Section your speech into segments and work out when you will employ pauses, increase pace, place emphasis and so forth. Make sure to time your speech when rehearsing, so you know how long it will take to complete in its entirety and how long each topic will take. Know where you should be every thirty seconds. Repetition is important, as by practising your speech you should form a 'mental clock' in your mind and you will become familiar with the progression of your speech.

The impact of nerves during delivery will inevitably take up more time than you realise, so bear this in mind during rehearsal. Never change the delivery and timing of your speech during the performance – stick to what you have done.

Organisation

For any public speaker, preparation is vital. After considering all the questions about audience, purpose and situation, you should ask:

- When does the event begin?
- When are you expected to arrive?
- For how long are you expected to speak?
- How far do you have to travel?
- What is the dress code?

Asking these questions will increase your host's opinion of your professionalism and will enhance your reputation.

Give yourself plenty of time for **travelling**. Take down the correct address and ask for directions both for private and public transport. Note in your diary what time you need to leave home to reach your venue with plenty of time; make allowances for delays on public transport or traffic problems. It is far better to arrive too early than too late.

When **preparing** your speech, keep your notes in one folder so you can refer to them and add to them as you research the topic or have a new idea. Avoid having research notes scattered in different places, as this will cause anxiety when you cannot find something that you consider to be very important. Keep a notebook with you to jot down ideas and new information.

Ensure that your speech is in **note form** and on note cards early on (do not leave this to the last minute). Then practise your speech from your notes and not a full written version. This will make you less worried about sticking to any specific wording and make your speech more spontaneous and relaxed. You may find it useful to create cue cards to aid you during your speech.

Preparation is the key to being organised and will boost your confidence: instead of being worried, you will look forward to sharing all your interesting information with your audience.

The venue

Ask questions about every important detail of the venue when you are first booked.

As soon as you arrive at the venue make yourself known to your hosts. Give yourself enough time to **check the room and the equipment** before the audience arrives. How big is the room? Are flip charts and plugs for electrical equipment available? Check where the electrical plugs are, then set up any equipment you need and any visual aids you have prepared.

Find out where you are expected to sit before you are announced, and where you will be speaking from. Go to these places and get the feel of the room. If possible, practise standing up and walking to the podium. Test the acoustics, and if you are expected to use a microphone then be sure to test that too.

Is there anywhere to put your notes and is the lighting good enough for you to see them? Will it be possible for the audience to see you (if possible, you want to be as brightly lit as possible)?

It is always better if you can visit the venue in advance to check these things but this is not always possible, so it is essential that you arrive in good time to do so on the day of your speech. This will enable you to sort out any potential problems and ensure a trouble-free event.

Bear in mind that you may be one of a series of speakers hired by the venue – for example, if you are speaking on a training day. If so, it will be unlikely that you can prepare ahead of the day. However, you should be aware of the equipment available to you, for your speech, before the day of the event. This should either be part of the initial conversation with the person who booked you or you can contact the venue and ask what will be provided in advance of the day.

Dress for success

The first thing your audience notices is you. Before they hear a word of what you say they have watched you: the way you are dressed, the way you move and your attitude. Personal presentation is very important and, therefore, you should pay attention to your grooming and your clothes should be neat and tidy. Try to avoid any elaborate or outrageous outfits, as in such cases the audience will be more aware of what you are wearing than what you are saying. Choose comfortable shoes that make you feel confident. Shoes will affect the way you stand, and that in turn will affect the way you breathe.

Structuring your Speech

The Roman orator Cicero studied the art of using language to persuade people. He produced rules that are still effective today. You first *invent* the speech (discussed in the previous section), then *arrange* it (discussed in this section), then you use good *memory*, *delivery* and *style* (examined in later chapters).

If you have not yet decided what your **message** is, look through your research and find the one thing that impresses you the most. Use that to define a clear message. This will help to fuel your enthusiasm for the speech, because you will want to find the best ways to share what you know, your ideas and your convictions. Keep your message in mind all the time.

Every effective speech must have a clear beginning, middle and end. In a coherent speech, these three elements must work together to bring the same message to the audience in a simple and memorable way.

Having collected the material for your speech, you now need to organise your material by selecting what will be interesting and appropriate to your audience, given the purpose and situation. Reject the material that is irrelevant or less interesting. Then arrange similar material into topics (or subdivisions). As you sift through the material, ask yourself, 'What will make a strong start to the speech? What will make an even stronger ending?'

Opening with impact

The opening of your speech should grab the attention of your listeners with an interesting, unusual or challenging statement related to your topic. The **introduction** serves several purposes. It must engage the audience and stimulate their interest. It gives the audience time to adjust to your appearance, voice and personality. It puts the audience in the right frame of mind.

(a) Firstly, **thank** the necessary people who might have been involved, like the organiser of the event, the performer who introduced you, or simply the audience for attending.

(b) Then establish **a link with the audience** by devising some common ground between you and them. For instance, a talk on home decorating could start with a rhetorical question: 'How many of you have tried to hang wallpaper to find it has indeed hung – everywhere except on the wall?' Nods from your audience will show that you have engaged them; you have begun with a subject that is of personal interest to the audience. If you can intrigue them at the same time, so much the better.

(c) You can **engage** your listeners by using one of the following gambits:

Startling statement: Make your audience sit up and listen. A talk on *Population Problems* could begin with 'For every second that I talk to you, three more babies have been born into this world. By the time I have finished, there will be over 10,000 more mouths to feed.'

Quotation: This is always a good beginning and one for which there are abundant sources. A well-known quotation establishes rapport with your audience if it is relevant to your speech and if it comes from someone they would consider an authority.

Story: This could be a short anecdote concerned with the subject. It might be a personal experience, which has prompted you to choose your topic for the speech. It is best to refer to something that has just happened.

Question: Ask a question, usually a rhetorical one, to interest, engage or inspire your audience. Use your audience research to frame a question that highlights what they need – the issue, which you will address in your speech.

Surprise: This is an excellent way of gaining attention at the start, but is obviously a bit risky! For example, if you were giving a speech on how valuable sight is you could present an image of a magnified iris or offer a surprising experience: 'Everyone, please close your eyes and listen to this recording. Tell me from which direction the truck is bearing down on you?' Whatever you do, it must be relevant to your speech.

Humour: Humour is hugely effective when it works. A humorous opening can be the best way of making an emotional connection. It requires a response from the audience, so when you get laughter it means the audience is involved. They will also pay attention for the next opportunity to laugh. You could use a short, sharp one-liner or a gentler story, or find an absurdity linked to your subject and exaggerate it. But this does not always work, so make sure you know the audience and their expectations before attempting this.

(d) **State your aim and clarify it:** Tell the audience in broad terms what your subject is.

For example: 'Tonight, I'd like to introduce you to the world of advertising and, in particular, to tell you about the methods of ensuring coverage of a product like this phone.'

(e) Identify the **main points** to be covered in the speech. This is an optional step and may appear to be unsubtle. Nevertheless, telling the audience what you are going to cover and how long it will take will convince them you know where the speech is going and you appreciate their time. The structure of your speech will be made clear at the outset – this is reassuring for both you and your listeners.

Reveal: Rather than quoting all the facts right at the beginning, the revealing opening keeps the audience guessing. Scatter your sentences with clues and draw the audience into your way of thinking. Beware, however, of asking too much of your audience at the start. If you are particularly confident, you could try an oblique opening where you set a false trail to make your audience guess where you might be going, which can engage and captivate an audience. You could, for instance, tell your audience all of the things you might have included, but have decided not to include on this occasion. Or you could show an unknown item, make a startling claim about it, and keep them guessing what it is by continuing your introduction with an apparently unrelated story.

Middles that move

To share your facts with the audience you must keep them interested. Your interest in your subject will help to bring the speech to life. The main body or middle of your speech needs to be constructed carefully so that you make a coherent argument. Unless you are speaking to experts on the subject, you will need to carry the audience on the back of a strong, logical sequence.

Use hooks to move the audience from one point to the next. A hook is a question that you promise to answer straight away. Ensure that the points you make follow a linear or sequential order, leading up to your strongest argument.

Divide your speech into the most relevant **topics**. Order the most important points within these topics, choosing the strongest ones. If you stick to this structure and limit yourself to three topics with three points under each, it will help to make your speech clear.

There must be a thread running through your speech and a sense of **development**. There are several methods to develop the body of your speech:

- Arrange the main points into a logical **time** sequence, without gaps (best for speeches where you're providing a historical timeline of events or looking at a person's life from birth to death).

- Discuss your subject from one **place** to another – for example, a speech about which cities to visit can be taken geographically from the UK to Europe and then to the rest of the world (best for subjects like travel or geography).

- Present every **part** of the whole subject. For instance, a speech about *The Senses* could be sub-divided into the use of the eyes, ears, nose, taste, touch and extra-sensory powers. In the same way, the various qualities or aspects of an object can be presented.

- Show **cause and effect**, either by describing a situation and then identifying the events leading up to it, or by naming a dramatic event and considering what the resulting consequences will be (speeches like *Why is our Water Polluted?* or *The World's Largest Volcanic Eruption*).

- **Compare and contrast** things by using their similarities and differences (a speech about *Fashion* could show what is happening in London, New York and Accra, showing what is the same in each city, and what is different).

- A persuasive speech is usually structured around a **problem and solution**. Present the problem, then all but one of the arguments that support your position in ascending order of importance. Finally, you refute (answer or discredit) the arguments advanced against you and then present the climax of your argument.

While strong material should be placed at the beginning and the end, the middle also needs some drama in it: passion, laughter or sympathy. Using **key words** relating to your main message will remind you and your audience what the speech is about.

Ending on a strong note

A strong ending stays in the minds of the listeners, leaving them satisfied, thoughtful or positive. Do not introduce new points. Aim to make your audience consider what you have said and end on a positive note.

Remind your audience of the main points. There is a good reason for the saying, 'Tell them what you are going to tell them, then tell them, and finally, tell them what you just told them.' There is nothing like repetition (using different words) for driving your point home!

Conclude the speech with a strong image that creates the mood you want. You could use a humorous remark, a startling statement, an emotional appeal, a relevant analogy to create a lasting impact or leave them with a story that pulls together many of the threads of what has gone before. Sum up the clear message of your speech and state what **action** the audience should take. Your speech often has a particular job to do (to propose a toast, to nominate someone or to declare a venue to be open).

Keep to your **time limit**. Avoid the temptation to fit in as many words as you possibly can into the time – allow for pausing and pace. Your audience will appreciate short pauses and moments of silence, so they can take in what you are saying before you move on to the next point.

To ensure the whole speech hangs together, the beginning, middle and ending must flow with direction and purpose. Martin Luther King repeated the phrase 'I have a dream', which provided a thread that will live in eternity in the minds of the free world. Now find yours!

Formal or informal?

Formal situations have rules and traditions that everyone is expected to follow, and there is often a dress code (for instance, black tie). Ceremonies and speeches are usually formal and require structured speeches with formal language (polite commentary, nothing too controversial and an educated choice of words).

Informal situations allow a more relaxed approach. The mood of the audience may be more casual, but most speaking appointments require the speaker to dress smartly. For small groups (fewer than six people) a chatty conversational style of presenting can often be used. For larger groups, a presentational style (using the techniques described in chapter *Structuring your speech*) helps you to make an impact.

Informal situations allow for more interaction than formal situations, so you should reduce the information you are planning to share to allow for the time taken by questions and responses. However, a clear structure is still necessary to get your message across. You need a beginning with impact, a moving middle and a strong ending.

Flow

Your speech should have one central message, but may be divided into various points or topics that help to reflect the purpose of the speech. You should change topic only when you have finished talking about the current topic. Do not come back to it later. Changing backward and forward between topics confuses the audience and weakens your structure.

When moving on to a new topic, introduce it with a link that explains how it relates to your central message. If, in the beginning, you outline the topics you will speak about, then the audience will understand how the new topic fits in to the speech. This keeps the speech flowing and carries your audience along with you.

Pace

You will have a time limit. Your audience have other things to do and you need to communicate your message without delay. A clear structure helps you to achieve this, by helping you to be efficient. The clearer your logic, the less time you need to explain what you mean. When each point has a strong link to your main message, your message has strong support and will be accepted sooner by the audience. Include only the information and examples that you need to present your message.

Speaking quickly does not help. It overloads your audience by presenting too much information too fast, and they may become confused or disinterested. The best way to make a quick speech is to speak slowly and clearly so the audience can follow you. Present less information, structured strongly around one message. Your audience will love you for it, because they will understand you.

If you are approaching your time limit and cannot complete what you prepared, do not speed up – simply skip one of your examples or topics. Never go beyond the time allowed.

How to shape subject matter into a concise speech – make it informative

When you watch a television news programme, as their objective is to inform the general public of current affairs in an unbiased and factual way, presenters use relevant facts and figures to support the point they wish to communicate. Facts are more effective when they come from a source the audience trust, so try to identify who they will consider to be an authority.

If you are not completely confident about the **key facts** you wish to convey to the audience, then do some more research to ensure you are speaking with accuracy and authority. Incorrect statements about a particular topic might cause the audience to doubt other aspects of your speech, and their trust in you as a communicator will be compromised. Accurate data enhances the audience's understanding of the information you are presenting.

To get your message across, express facts in terms familiar to the audience. For example, a statement that there are four million CCTV cameras in the UK is rather difficult to relate to. However, if you clarify the statement by saying: 'that is one camera for every fifteen people in the country', this makes things clear as it is easy for the audience to envisage.

Headings and key words

By organising your material you will discover the main headings for each division in your speech and the keywords that summarise the main points within each section. You could write these key words on cards to guide your train of thought. Deal with one point at a time, finish it and move on. That will help your audience to follow and remain involved.

By refining your script with headings and key words you can avoid the trap of having to read your entire speech, which shows poor preparation and presentation skills. Having the entire text of your original speech on cards makes it difficult to read, causing you to hold the cards closer and closer to your face until the audience can't see you at all. It is far better to have a clear and simple structure outlined on a few cards so you can concentrate on maintaining eye contact with your audience and displaying spontaneity in your delivery.

Express an opinion

When you speak about your own experiences and convictions you make your speech unique and interesting. Expressing a few personal opinions in a constructive way, grounded in fact, can be good. However, too much opinion in a speech makes it *opinionated*. People like to be informed and inspired rather than to be lectured. Take great care not to use the word 'I' too much, as this will alienate the audience and damage the sense of sharing that is so important during communication.

Display in-depth knowledge

Your audience will soon detect whether your knowledge is in-depth or not. If you have taken the time to study the topic and know it intimately, then you will have the confidence to communicate your knowledge in depth and detail.

A good strategy is to cite examples that help make a particular point more relevant in a different way and improve the audience's understanding. A picture paints a thousand words; the use of an effective example may do the same. Think of real cases you have observed, and what you believe those cases demonstrate.

By using a specific example that is relevant to the point you are making, you will often clarify and enhance the listener's understanding of the topic, and some of the points you have made may stick in their minds long after the speech is over.

Justify your argument

If you decide to present an argument on a particular subject, then strong evidence will be needed to justify your position and to avoid an impression of bias. The audience will not be convinced with weak reasons for your arguments, so find your **evidence** first and base your arguments upon it. Use facts from trusted sources.

Avoid the overuse of statistics, as it can be a lot of information for your audience to take in.

To increase the impact of your main points, you can restate them during the course of your speech, but try not to be too repetitive. Saying the same point in different ways can help with this – for example, if you're talking about the best play in London, you can say '*the best play is…*', '*the most successful play is…*', '*the play with the best reviews is…*' and so forth.

A clear viewpoint

A single viewpoint supported by strong arguments can produce a brief and effective speech. If you have a short time limit you may be unable to give a balanced argument in which you discuss both sides of an issue, or investigate many different viewpoints.

If you decide that there is a need to present differing viewpoints, manage them carefully to ensure a fair and consistent treatment. A balanced argument means presenting both sides, so that the members of the audience are fully briefed on all aspects of the case and as a result of this information, can make up their own minds. In other words, they make an informed decision that is without bias or prejudice.

Propaganda and polemic should be avoided, as these can alienate the audience. If you wish to communicate a personal viewpoint, then do so openly, making your position clear and stating why you believe you are correct. Balance, and not bias, is what most audiences will respect.

Work within a time limit

Time your speech when you rehearse, so you can be certain you will meet the time limit. The audience will come to listen to a speech about a topic that presumably interests them, but they are busy people. No matter how short the time seems to you, aim to finish promptly. Leave them wanting more, rather than wanting you to stop talking.

If your preparation time is limited, as with an impromptu speech, define the structure of your speech right away. Choose your topic. Establish your key themes: you can now outline them in your beginning and summarise them in your ending. Divide the themes into main points and select the strongest ones. Add a relevant opening and memorable closing remark – an impromptu speech must also end with impact. In the time remaining, you can develop each point to be clear and concise.

Common speech styles

A useful guiding principle to shape your speech is **style**. Style can be most conspicuous by its absence – a clear and appropriate style will give your speech power, and it should be influenced by the mood you wish to create.

The persuasive speech

Convince the audience that your point of view is correct. To do this you need to use a valid argument, which is structured using key facts linked in a logical progression.

State your facts, illustrate them, argue from the facts and finally appeal for action.

Identify the **problem** that the audience faces, and show the audience the benefit of agreeing with you. The more relevant the topic is to the audience, the easier it will be to persuade them. It is best to begin your logical journey on the **common ground** that you share with the audience.

For instance, if you are trying to persuade members of the student union to stop smoking, you might begin with 'Are you afraid of dying? Well, I'm afraid of dying, too.' Then identify the problem that the audience faces (smoking can cause cancer and premature death) and the **benefit** of stopping (a healthy life). The benefit answers the question 'Why should we listen to this speech?' Find out who your audience would regard as an **authority** and use quotes and arguments made by public figures or heroes they respect.

Support your logical journey with indisputable scientific **facts**. Use positive arguments for your case and show how your points are better than any criticisms raised against them, in a way that makes sense to your audience. Lastly, show them how they can take action. For instance, 'Heroes take **action**. Are you a hero? Quit today, right now, by throwing out all your cigarettes.'

The informative speech

Educate the audience with interesting and useful information. It must be relevant to them, so the starting point here is audience research. The speech must be supported by clear presentation.

This is the most common type of speech that you will have to make. In a minor way, you make one every time you give instructions or provide information in a conversation on the telephone. The informative speech can be a **narration** (*My Most Frightening Experience*), a **description** (*The Himalayas*) or an **exposition** (*Maintaining Your Car*).

These are not exclusive divisions. A speech about your holiday could include an exposition on how you prepared for the journey, a description of the venue and a narration of the day-to-day events. However, the following principles must be observed when giving an informative speech:

- facts must be presented in a logical manner
- there should be no provocation or argument in the content
- the speaker should present the facts without bias.

The objective of an informative speech is to generate interest, to inform and stimulate curiosity within the audience. A useful way to begin your preparation is to outline the speech as follows:

Subject	your working title
General purpose	to inform, narrate or describe?
Specific purpose	the nature of your speech (an account, a description, a story, an exposition, an outline of a policy, or a host of other things)
Audience	your listeners (age, gender, educational background or experience, occupation, social habits, special interests, prejudices and attitudes)
Situation	why the talk is being given

So, for example:

Subject	Nomadic lifestyles
General purpose	to inform
Specific purpose	to describe the life of nomadic people – the benefits, hardships and public opinion
Audience	mixed, but consisting of publishers and those in the industry
Situation	Book launch at a book fair

This assumes you have been asked to give your speech on a specific subject. If the choice is up to you, choose a topic that will be relevant to your audience. Limit the scope of the subject according to the time available. You could think of a general title and list all of its sub-divisions against it. For example:

GENERAL TITLE	POSSIBLE SUB-DIVISIONS
	– Analysis
	– Sources
	– Natural uses
	– Bodily uses

If we looked at a 'General Title' of water, this could be sub-divided as follows:

Water	– Circulation
	– Industrial uses
	– Household uses
	– Purification
	– Distribution

Obviously the subject 'Water' is much too general to cover in detail in a single speech. Nine sub-divisions have been created and there are more possibilities.

Next you should take a sub-division and further expand that. For example, if the general title is 'Water', a sub-division could be 'Circulation', then further sub-divisions are possible:

	– In nature
Circulation	– In plants
	– In animals

Even the extent of this sub-division may be too crowded, since an hour's speech could be given on the water cycle in nature only: rain > streams > rivers > sea > water vapour > clouds > rain.

Similarly, the use of water by plants could open up wide possibilities concerning content – osmosis, transportation in xylem, use in photosynthesis, transpiration and so on. In fact, with the more learned, scientifically minded audiences each of these topics could easily be developed into a whole lecture or a series of lectures.

Once you have chosen your subject, do some reading about it. Research is invaluable to aid confidence, assurance and authority. Make notes on the points you would like to cover and write each on a separate card. Once you feel that you have enough material, begin to sift out that which is extraneous or distracting. Avoid introducing open-ended facts; they divert the attention of your audience onto avenues that you are not going to explore.

Using one card for one topic enables you to rearrange the content of your speech until you feel the order is the best one. Check the order for logical and neat transitions from fact to fact.

The political speech

Motivate the audience to take your side on an issue of public interest. As the issue is probably controversial and often emotive, you will need to be certain of your facts, so base them on current research. (For a detailed example, refer to our chapter *Case studies*.)

The humorous speech

Entertain the audience while leading them on a journey to make a point. Humour relies on skilled delivery and wit that matches the audience. It is difficult to do well. The speech must have an underlying purpose or it will lack impact. Humour works well when it is relevant to the audience, based on experiences they can relate to.

The impromptu speech

Engage the audience on a topic with little or no preparation. A clear structure is important: a good beginning, a middle section with linked ideas, and a strong ending to wrap everything up.

Sometimes you are expected to talk on a given topic with very little preparation time.

Use this preparation time well. Explore the potential of each topic offered, selecting the one best suited to you, your relevant knowledge, experience or interests, and begin to write your ideas in note form. A clear structure is important. Allow time to practise the speech to ensure it is long enough, matching your tone, style and content to your intended audience.

Your notes are merely an aid for your memory and could, therefore, be a single paragraph with headings or key words. You must not read from your notes because it is vital to engage your audience with eye contact.

As you prepare, imagine the venue for your speech. When beginning your speech, introduce yourself and your topic to the audience – state your purpose. Engage your audience with eye contact.

The vote of thanks

Address the audience with a short conclusion to the main speaker's address.

T H A N K is a simple mnemonic to help you remember the steps in giving a vote of thanks.

T: Title contrast – if possible, try to express the original title of the speech in another way. Suppose the speech is on Flower Arrangement; a suitable title contrast would be *How Can Flowers Grace Your Home?* The person giving the introduction announces the title, and the speaker dwells on the subject. Therefore, it is more imaginative to rephrase the title of the speech.

H: Highlight – select the item of particular relevance from the speech that stands out in your memory. Make only a brief reference to this.

A: Add – enhance the highlight with something from your own experience. Take care that you do not make another speech and that you support what the speaker has established.

N: Nice – say something nice about the speaker, without being patronising.

K: Key closing words – do not use phrases like 'I think' or 'I feel sure'; be positive, say something like: 'I know you will join me in extending a most sincere thank you to our speaker,' followed by personal thanks: 'Mr Speaker, your speech was illuminating, I enjoyed it immensely and look forward to welcoming you back after your journey to Antarctica.' Look at the speaker when doing so.

Although every speech has an overall style, an interesting and well-constructed speech will contain elements of a number of the above styles, to suit the topic and to enhance the mood of a particular moment. Variety will interest the audience, as will the well-timed use of contrast in content and delivery.

Other speech styles

There are many other speech styles to explore in your own time. For example, an **acceptance speech** expresses your gratitude for the award with a brief address that compliments the host organisation and their achievements. A **tribute** shows respect for someone and expresses your thanks. A tribute can also be an informative speech. An **inspiring speech** convinces the audience that they can succeed. A **motivational speech** makes the audience take action to improve their situation.

try this

Select a topic that you're familiar with and practise presenting it in different speech styles; for example, a humorous, impromptu, inspiring and motivational speech on the benefits of exercise.

Enhancing your speech

Your speech can be enhanced to suit your audience by using quotations and humour, creating contrast and using literary techniques such as sound patterning.

Using quotations and humour

Using a **quotation** to underline the point you are trying to make helps the audience to understand and remember what you are saying. It must not appear contrived, but needs to flow as naturally as possible, arising spontaneously from the content and context of your speech.

The possibilities for quotations are endless, from William Shakespeare to Mahatma Gandhi, or even those closer to home. The best quotes are from people the audience respect.

Humour is a wonderful strategy to make an audience feel relaxed and entertained. Laughter can sometimes be the only opportunity for the audience to participate in a speech. Laughter wakes your audience up and they will pay closer attention to you, as they look for the next opportunity to laugh. This is why beginning a speech with a humorous anecdote or quotation is a common and successful strategy.

Timing is important because if judged wrongly the humour can fall flat and be embarrassing. Practise with some friends before presenting what you think is humorous.

Anecdotal humour (an apparently spontaneous aside to the audience) works well if it is appropriate. You bring the audience into your world, allowing them to share the funny side of a predicament in which you found yourself. Use this strategy sparingly or your speech will be too personal and lacking in useful information.

Pause for laughter, but if there is none continue immediately as if you were not expecting any – there is nothing worse than a speaker criticising an audience for their poor sense of humour, or having to explain a joke.

Both quotations and humour will make the audience more receptive, but only when relevant to the audience. Base your quotations and humour on your research into the audience, which should help you to identify things they would find humorous and subjects they consider taboo. You should not make a joke that is not politically correct – avoid jokes that would offend anyone present or any group of people (especially based on religion, race or gender).

Creating contrast

A **contrast** is a comparison showing striking differences. Your point can have more impact if you create a contrast around it by presenting extremely different examples. For example, tell the story of how one friend failed and another succeeded. Show the bad effects of the alternative and the good effects of your solution. Present the horror of the oppressed, then the wonder of their freedom after liberation. Make sure the contrast reinforces the point you are trying to make.

Preparing different content for two speeches might make them both interesting, but to make them truly dynamic they need contrast. Creating contrast between speeches can demonstrate your ability as a speaker and indicate your progression in developing communication skills. Matching the content and delivery of your speech to different audiences in different situations, with a different sense of purpose, shows sensitivity.

You communicate more effectively with an audience if you use a style of speech and language with which they feel comfortable.

This offers a further opportunity to develop contrast between your speeches. For example, you could pitch your first speech to a group of sceptical scientists (who may respond better to intellectual argument and specialised terminology) and the second speech to young sports fans (who may respond better to passionate opinions and simple language).

Sound patterning

Writers and speakers can use a range of devices for playing on the patterns and sounds of words to create certain stylistic effects. These are chosen to enhance the meaning to be conveyed to the audience.

Alliteration

Alliteration is the repetition of a consonant, often in the initial position:

- Pick up a Penguin

In advertisements, captions and headlines, this device can be used to make the text more eye-catching and memorable.

Alliteration can also be used effectively in poetry:

> Let us not speak of those days
>
> when coffee beans filled the morning
>
> with *hope*, when our mothers' *headscarves*
>
> *hung* like white flags on washing lines.

> Tishani Doshi,
> *The River of Girls*

Consonance

Consonance is the repetition of a consonant in the final position:

- Bea*nz* Mea*nz* Hei*nz*

This device can draw attention to a product name in advertising, or enhance the meaning of literary language by the repeated, sharp sound.

Assonance

Assonance is the repetition of a vowel in the middle position (an element that does not occur in the initial or the first position):

The pallor of girls' brows shall be their pall;

Their flowers the tenderness of patient minds,

And each slow dusk a drawing-down of blinds.

> Wilfred Owen (1893–1918),
> *Anthem for Doomed Youth*

This poetic device makes words sound sonorous and musical, and is often used to create a grave or pensive tone.

Onomatopoeia

Onomatopoeia is the term used when the sound of a word suggests its meaning.

It *SHUSHES*

It *hushes*

The loudness in the road.

It flitter-twitters,

And laughs away from me.

> Gwendolyn Brooks (1917–2000),
> *Cynthia in the Snow*

The emphasis on the sound of the words reinforces the image you are trying to create.

Rhyme

Rhyme or half-rhyme are exact or partial repetitions of a sound, usually at the end of a poetic line:

> Does the road wind up-hill all the way?
>
> Yes, to the very *end*.
>
> Will the day's journey take the whole long day?
>
> From morn to night, my *friend*.
>
>> Christina Rossetti (1830–1894),
>> *Up-Hill*

This kind of sound patterning can be used to draw attention to certain words. It creates a kind of end focus and can be used in a conclusive way to emphatically signal the end of a poem or speech.

Figures of speech

A figure of speech (literary device) is a word or phrase with a specialised meaning not based on its literal meaning. Such language is an important part of successful persuasion because it allows a speaker to combine everyday words with devices that create special effects. For example, when presenting the benefits of studying, you could say that students are 'climbing the ladder to success', which reinforces the idea of structured learning with the image of a useful supportive device that allows you to reach higher than you can on your own. There are many figures of speech.

Irony

Irony is the use of a word, phrase or paragraph turned from its usual meaning to a contradictory or opposing one, usually to satirise or deflate the person or issue:

> I do therefore humbly offer it to public consideration that of the hundred and twenty thousand children already computed, twenty thousand may be reserved for breed [...] That the remaining hundred thousand may, at a year old, be offered in the sale to the persons of quality and fortune through the kingdom; always advising the mother to let them

suck plentifully in the last month, so as to render them plump and fat for a good table. A child will […] make a reasonable dish, and seasoned with a little pepper or salt will be very good boiled on the fourth day, especially in winter.

Jonathan Swift (1667–1745),
A Modest Proposal for preventing the children of poor people in Ireland from being a burden to their parents or country, and for making them beneficial to the public

In this text, Swift adopts an ironic stance, suggesting that eating babies is the only way to tackle Ireland's problems of poverty and overpopulation. By making such an emotive proposal, Swift aims to draw attention to the failures of both England and Ireland in governing and providing for the people. When using irony, make sure that the audience can recognise that the technique is being used, especially if you are addressing an international audience.

Metaphor

A metaphor describes one thing in terms of another, creating a comparison:

Remember that *I am thy creature; I ought to be thy Adam, but I am rather the fallen angel*, whom thou drivest from joy for no misdeed.

Mary Wollstonecraft (Godwin) Shelley (1797–1851),
Frankenstein; or, the Modern Prometheus

Here Frankenstein is speaking to his creator. He compares his creator to God and he, instead of being Adam – the creation of God – is a fallen angel.

However, it is only effective when it is not a mixed metaphor – an illogical association between two unrelated concepts. For example, when a freedom-of-speech activist is exposed in the newspapers for lying, someone might be tempted to say that 'the sacred cows have come home to roost'. A 'sacred cow' is unreasonably immune from criticism (his zealous belief in freedom of speech); 'coming home to roost' means something has unfavourable repercussions.

Personification

Personification is the term used when an object or idea is given human qualities. An example of this can be seen in the poem *Because I could not stop for Death* by Emily Dickinson (1830–1886), where death is personified:

> Because I could not stop for Death –
> *He kindly stopped for me* –
> The Carriage held but just Ourselves –
> And Immortality.

Simile

In a simile two things are explicitly compared by using a marker such as the preposition 'like' or 'as':

> When the others spoke their voices swept over us like bees hovering over lilacs.
>
> J. Mae Barizo,
> *The Women*

Oxymoron

An oxymoron uses two apparently contradictory words put together to create a special effect, like 'delicious poison', or 'Robin Hood was an honest thief'.

Paradox

A paradox consists of an apparently self-contradictory statement, which contains some kind of deeper meaning below the surface. For instance, in his book *1984*, George Orwell (1903–1950) wrote 'War is peace. Freedom is slavery.'

Symbolism

Symbolism is the use of an object to represent or stand for something else – *scales*, for instance, symbolise *justice*; a *dove* symbolises *peace*.

Metonymy and Synecdoche

Metonymy is the term used when the name of an associated aspect is substituted for the thing itself. For instance, *the stage* means the theatrical profession. In a similar way, synecdoche is when a part stands for the whole: 'The prisoner was placed behind bars' (meaning in prison).

All of these devices allow writers and speakers to influence their audience's perceptions of the subject. By encouraging readers and listeners to make wider associations, writers and speakers can work on their emotions and can also convey their own viewpoint in a more personal way.

Structural devices

To successfully persuade an audience, you can use devices to enhance your meaning and to structure your speech. There are many techniques that can be useful in this regard, and combining them can create an even greater impact.

Antithesis

Antithesis is placing two words or ideas in opposition to create a *contrast*:

It was the *best of times*,

it was the *worst of times*,

it was the *age of wisdom*,

it was the *age of foolishness*,

it was the *epoch of belief*,

it was the *epoch of incredulity*,

it was the *season of Light*,

it was the *season of Darkness*,

it was the *spring of hope*,

it was the *winter of despair*,

   Charles Dickens (1812–1870),
   A Tale of Two Cities

Antithesis can be used to show a contradiction or a comparison, or to present opposites, such as: *We must learn to live together as brothers or perish together as fools*, Martin Luther King, Jr. (1929–1968).

Listing

It is easy to think about many items when they are grouped together with similar items in a list. However, if the list is too long, your audience may have forgotten what the first item was by the time you get to the last one, and you lose the impact created by repetition and support. An effective list is one of **three**. Three things clustered together are easy to remember. It is the shortest list that seems complete, and helps to convey a sense of progress. You can use three different words, three phrases, or three sentences to support one point. This technique is often used in public speaking: *I came, I saw, I conquered*, Julius Caesar.

Listing always has a cumulative effect and enables a writer or speaker to create a range of impressions. A long list can convey confusion and chaos or logic and reason, depending on its context. Equally, a writer or speaker can build towards a climax, or defy expectations by concluding with an anti-climax.

[1] Only you can see, in the blinded bedrooms, the combs and petticoats over chairs, the jugs and basins, the glasses of teeth, the 'Thou Shalt Not' on the wall, and the yellowing dickybird-watching pictures of the dead. [2] Only you can hear and see, behind the eyes of the sleepers, the movements and countries and mazes and colours and dismays and rainbows and tunes and wishes and flight and fall and despairs and big seas of their dreams.

Dylan Thomas (1914–1953),
Under Milk Wood

In this example, Thomas uses listing in both sentences, but the effect achieved in each case is different. In sentence [1] the accumulation of objects creates a claustrophobic atmosphere, which mirrors the everyday lives of the inhabitants of Llareggub. In sentence [2], however, the repeated use of the conjunction 'and' creates a sense of the freedom that the inhabitants find in the limitless nature of their dreams.

Overstatement

Overstatement or *hyperbole* is a form of persuasive exaggeration:

> Prettier musings of *high-wrought love* and *eternal constancy* could never have passed along the streets of Bath, than Anne was sporting from Camden Place to Westgate Buildings. It was almost enough to *spread purification* and *perfume* all the way.
>
> > Jane Austen (1775–1817),
> > *Persuasion*

Austen's use of hyperbole here results in a parody (a comic imitation) of contemporary romantic novels. Exaggeration of this kind will often be adopted to create a comic or less-than-serious tone.

Understatement

Understatement or *litotes* allows the audience to recognise that the writer or speaker could have put the point more strongly.

> I have, myself, full confidence that if all do their duty, if nothing is neglected, and if the best arrangements are made…we shall prove ourselves once again able to defend our island home, to ride out the storm of war, and to outlive the menace of tyranny… At any rate, that is what we are going to try to do…
>
> > Winston Churchill (1874–1965)

There are two distinct tones here: the initially grand and very formal tone and the italicised informal one. The contrast between these suggests that the second sentence has been understated – Churchill could have said much more.

Puns

A pun is a play upon words for a humorous effect. Puns can be words that have different meanings but the same sound. Newspaper headlines often play with words to attract attention. The following headline was about the possibility of fires in the Channel Tunnel:

Burning questions on tunnel safety unanswered.

The pun is in the words 'burning questions'. The questions are about fires, hence burning questions, but a 'burning question' can also mean an important or urgent question.

When is an ambulance not an ambulance?

When it turns into a hospital!

Here 'turns into' can mean *changes* into or *turns a corner* into.

Take care to use only puns that are relevant in your speech and use them sparingly, or you will cause your audience to groan instead of laugh.

Repetition

Repetition of words, phrases, clauses or sentences draws attention to key ideas:

Your £15 gift can help the children so much

Your £15 can help us to maintain our family care

Your £15 can help to cover the cost of counselling a traumatised child

Your £15 can help fund our Child Protection Helpline

Your £15 can help a child whose life may be in danger

NSPCC Christmas Appeal leaflet (October 1995)

The repetition of the noun phrase *Your £15* and the verb phrase *can help* emphasises that donations do not have to be large – to many people £15 is a nominal sum of money, yet it enables the charity to provide a wide range of services. The repetition is persuasive because it is emotive – so little can achieve so much.

Sentence structure

A varied choice of sentence types will draw the reader or listener into the discourse. A writer or speaker must think about the use of simple, complex and branching sentences.

Simple sentences can suggest an innocence and a naivety of style:

> 'This is a chair for me. I am sure of it because it is so high. How quickly it was made!' said the child, full of admiration and wonder.

> Johanna Spyri (1827–1901),
> Heidi

The simple sentences here portray a style that is reminiscent of a child – Heidi, the main character of the story, who is the speaker.

Complex sentences can withhold information until a certain point in the discourse or subordinate some ideas to others that seem more important:

> We shall all agree that the fundamental aspect of the novel is its story-telling aspect, but we shall voice our assent in different tones, and it is on the precise tone of voice which we employ now that our subsequent conclusions will depend.

> E. M. Forster (1879–1970),
> Aspects of the Novel

Rhetorical questions

Rhetorical questions come in various forms. Here are some of the ways you can use them:

(a) a question that requires no answer because it expresses a truth which cannot be denied (for example, Are we alive?)

(b) a question to which we immediately supply our own answer (for example, Do we want to stay alive? Yes we do!)

(c) a string of questions uttered in rapid succession for the sake of emotional emphasis (for example, Will we live when all the seas are empty of fish? Will we live when all the rivers are poisoned? Will we live when the sky is filled with pollution and the only rain is acid?)

(d) An enquiry in a tone of bewilderment or amazement and allowing no satisfactory or easy reply (for example, after (c), Then what are we doing?)

Rhetorical questions are a useful way to break up the monotony of a speech and to engage the audience. In effect, you are making them ask a question, so they will listen closely to the answer. For example, in the midst of your speech you could say, 'You ask what proof I have that it is so? I have overwhelming evidence. Firstly…'

Memorising your speech

Your speech will have more impact if it appears to be spontaneous, so it should come from memory rather than from a script.

Some people are lucky; they seem to remember things with no trouble at all. Others need to work hard, especially if they have left the writing of the speech to the last minute. But if you prepare your work in advance, memorising the relevant parts of your speech will be easier.

When preparing a shorter speech, or one for examination purposes, write out the key points of your speech but **do not write it out word for word**. A clear structure, with headings and keywords, will help you to remember it.

When preparing a lengthy lecture or an official speech it may be helpful to write out your full speech first to clarify your ideas and to give an accurate indication of the length of the whole speech when spoken aloud. Then you can improve the grammar, vocabulary, sentence structure and logic.

Summarise your speech on **note cards**. Put each theme on a separate card to reduce the information. Include your main points, all key words and important passages or quotes, but keep it brief. Note cards are there only to remind you of your key points.

An alternative to note cards is an **outline sheet**, which shows the entire speech at one glance, listing only the beginning and ending statements, the main headings and key words. However, you must take care that this remains on your lectern. If you hold it in front of you it becomes a barrier between you and your audience. Index cards are useful, as they sit unobtrusively in your hand.

Try to memorise the important parts only, like your introduction and conclusion, any quotes and the key words and headings. Do not try to memorise the entire body text – your message is more important than the words you use to share it.

If you struggle to remember your speech, it may be a sign that you need to simplify your subject matter. You may be trying to get across too much detailed information. Focus on your inspiring **message** and not the exact words you will use.

Finally, and most importantly, **practise** your speech, because memory is improved by regular repetition.

You can divide your speech into manageable sections and practise saying those aloud to your imagined audience. Repeat this until you have the confidence to use only the headings and key words on your cards. Practise managing the cards in your hands, because they can distract the listeners' attention if handled badly. You can practise a particular section in all sorts of places – while travelling in the car, or going for a walk. As your memory improves you will be able to handle more of the speech in one go.

The important thing is to practise aloud, not only in your mind. To ensure your delivery remains spontaneous and fresh, change your pace, pitch and pausing to enhance the meaning and mood. Experiment with projecting your voice and exploring your own range of expression. If you have prepared and practised, you will have the confidence and skill to communicate well.

Visual aids can be very useful to help you remember the points you want to make. For example, a speech about football can include a poster of your favourite football team, which will help you to remember the key players as you discuss each in turn. For a speech about dancing you could present a costume, dancing shoes, a cup you won at a dancing competition and a postcard from Cork where you saw the best dancer. Objects can be used to remind you of sections in your speech. Similarly, the images in a PowerPoint presentation will remind you of your linked ideas, so practise looking at the images and recalling what you want to say about each one.

Visual memory

Another method to help you to memorise the speech is to create visual stories using headings and key words. For example, assuming you had a speech on global environmental damage, one of your cards might be the destruction of rainforests, divided into your main points of:

- Where were trees destroyed?
- What caused it?
- What was the hidden cost?

Let us assume you have data to show that between 1990 and 2005, 3% of all forests were lost and that currently over 30 million acres a year (more than half of the area of Great Britain, or more than one acre per second) are lost. You also have data to show that within this 3%, the biggest percentage loss of forests occurred in Africa (9%) and Latin America (6%). These figures are illustrative and close to the truth. But how can you possibly remember all those facts?

You could start by drawing a picture of three large trees, shaped like Africa, the World, and Latin America. Put the numbers nine, three and six in the head of each tree to signify the percentage of their forests lost. It would help to make the 9% tree taller than the others, and the world tree, although shortest at 3%, round and fat, to remind you that it is the world tree. You might use illustrations to remind you that there is one acre of trees lost every second. For example, you could write 'Britain' beneath the world tree, and slash the word in half to remind you that more than half the area of Great Britain is lost from world forests per year.

The major causes can be placed at the base of the trees – firstly a person tending flames to signify slash-and-burn subsistence farming, secondly a cow with a dollar sign on it to signify commercial farming, lastly a pile of logs to signify logging. The hidden cost, hidden above the forest in a low cloud, can be a speckled group of insects above the world tree (biodiversity) with the number 50,000 (the number of species that become extinct every year). A medicine bottle, quarter full, signifies that 25% of the world's plant-derived medicines come from forests as well as 25% of all cancer-curing medicines. Then a person labelled 'million' in a circle, with three-quarters of the person shaded out, could show the loss of indigenous people since 1900, a population of one million that is now only 250,000.

Make up your own unique picture. Because you invented it, the image is unique and easy to remember. Images are easier to remember because your visual memory is often more powerful and effective than your factual memory. Use it to your advantage by drawing pictures that tell your story and see if you prefer them to your note cards. You can add graphic elements to the image, but limit it to one theme or you may get confused.

Vocal techniques

Research tells us that we are much more affected by the delivery of words than by the words themselves. So, you can prepare a written speech meticulously but when you deliver your speech if your voice and body language don't do their jobs effectively, you will not be successful. Perhaps you should keep in mind that it's not what you say but the way that you say it!

In this chapter, we will consider the vocal techniques required for making speeches. We will look at warming up your voice and building your projection skills.

How your voice works

An understanding of how your voice works will help you to develop your ability to project your voice.

Breathing

There are many bones, muscles and nerves involved in breathing:

Bones: Your spine is made up of a series of vertebrae. Your ribs curve around from the vertebrae to the front of your chest forming the ribcage where most ribs join at the sternum. You can feel the definition of the ribs with your fingers.

Muscles: Your *intercostal muscles* are situated between your ribs ('inter' means between and 'costal' means ribs). The *diaphragm* is a dome-shaped muscle dividing the chest and the abdomen. It is attached to the lower edges of the ribcage, the point of the sternum and the vertebrae. The *abdominal muscles* help to control the movement of the diaphragm in the abdominal cavity.

Breathing in: Your intercostal muscles contract and move your ribs slightly upwards and outwards. The diaphragm, attached to the ribs, moves in response to this and flattens out. This creates more space inside the chest, giving the lungs room to expand. As the lungs expand, the air pressure reduces. Air immediately flows in through the nose or mouth to equalise the pressure. Your abdominal muscles release and your lungs fill with air.

Breathing out: When you exhale, the same muscles converge on your lungs to support the release of the breath. The abdominal muscles contract, the diaphragm rises and the ribcage returns to its original position through the relaxation of the intercostal muscles. Your lungs are compressed and air flows out through your nose and mouth, powered by your abdominal muscles.

Breath support: To 'support your voice' means having the right amount of pressure from the abdominal muscles to create the right amount of breath force for the sound you want to use. For example, if you want to project your voice across a large space or to sustain a long phrase, then you will need a more consistent pressure from your abdominal muscles. Taking breath from your 'centre' (an imaginary point inside your body below your navel) will also help you to relax and release the sound. Refer to chapter *Practice, practice, practice!* for helpful breathing exercises.

Clavicular breathing: This is a mistake that occurs when you move your ribs upwards but not outwards when breathing in, holding air in your upper lungs and raising your shoulders. This sometimes happens when your body is tense, and it puts strain on your vocal cords. Make sure that your spine is lengthened and your shoulders, neck and jaw are free from tension. Pause, take a deep breath that goes deep down into your abdomen, then speak.

Voice production

As you breathe in, the diaphragm contracts, which causes air to flow in through the mouth or nose, pass down the windpipe (trachea) and into the lungs. As you breathe out, the diaphragm relaxes and the abdominal muscles work to return breath up the trachea, where it passes the voice box (larynx). The larynx is a protective valve for the airway. When you close the vocal cords across the air flow it makes sounds because the edges of the cords vibrate. The short edges of the vocal cords vibrate very rapidly.

Figure 1: The larynx (from the side)

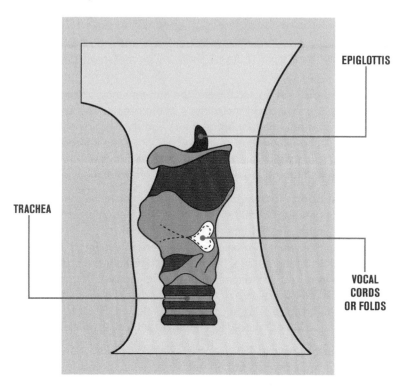

EPIGLOTTIS

TRACHEA

VOCAL
CORDS
OR FOLDS

Figure 2: The larynx (from the above)

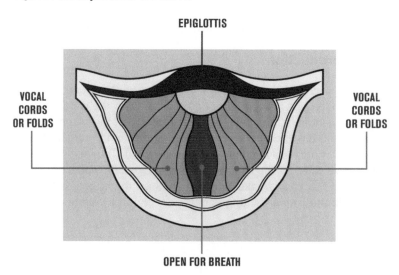

EPIGLOTTIS

VOCAL
CORDS
OR FOLDS

VOCAL
CORDS
OR FOLDS

OPEN FOR BREATH

Speech

Voice is the sound that is made when the breath passes over the vocal bands and then is enlarged or amplified in the hollow cavities (resonators). Sound is turned into **speech** by using the speech organs (the tongue, the teeth, the teeth ridge and the hard and soft palates) to shape the sound into words to give it articulation.

Words are made up of consonants and vowels. A vowel is formed by changing the shape of the mouth without obstructing the sound. A consonant is formed by the use of the speech organs to obstruct the sound. To be sure that your speech is clear, it is important that these speech organs are used correctly.

Sometimes a weakness in one or other of the speech organs can lead to unclear speech. Exercises to strengthen the lips and the tongue can help to overcome many of these weaknesses, but they must be done regularly if they are going to produce clearer speech. Refer to chapter *Practice, practice, practice!* for some examples.

Resonance

Resonance is the amplification of sound achieved through vibration. The quality of the sound is deep, full and reverberating. An echo is an example of this. A noise in a cave will be amplified, as the sound travels through the cave and reverberates in the empty space creating an echo.

Vocal resonance refers to the amplification of sound waves as they pass through the hollow spaces of the pharynx, mouth and nose. These sound waves are produced by the vibrating vocal folds of the larynx. These vibrations create a small sound in the larynx, which is then amplified, strengthened and given texture as it reverberates in the three hollow spaces of the neck and head.

Primary resonators

- pharynx (pharyngeal resonator, which extends upwards from the larynx)
- mouth (oral resonator)
- nose (nasal resonator)

Secondary resonators

- head resonance (used primarily for softer singing)
- chest resonance (adds richer, darker and deeper tone)

The quality of resonance changes depending on how strong or weak the breath force is and how the speaker shapes and tenses the resonators. If the breath force is strong enough, the sound carried from the pharynx into the mouth will bounce off the hard palate and out through the lips – this is called forward resonance.

If the breath force is weak, the sound may not reach the hard palate, pitching only onto the soft palate, making vocal projection difficult.

The pharynx (pharyngeal resonator) is the long muscular tube, which extends upwards from the larynx, ending at the back part of the oral and nasal cavities. It is the first resonating space through which the note passes on its way to the mouth and nose.

The pharynx can change its shape and size, which affects the quality of the sound produced. It increases in size during a yawn and decreases in size when the throat or neck is tense.

 Hold a yawn in your throat and count 'one, two, three' at the same time. You will hear a sound with too much pharyngeal resonance.

The mouth (oral resonator): The many parts of the mouth each play a part in producing resonance.

The lower jaw forms the floor of the oral resonator and is attached to the facial bones by hinge joints.

The tongue lies on the floor of the oral resonator, rooted in the front wall of the pharynx. It is capable of intricate and rapid movements. The movement is centred in different areas: the tip (point of the tongue), the blade (underneath the upper tooth ridge), the front (underneath the hard palate), the centre (partly underneath the hard palate and partly underneath the soft palate) and the back (underneath the soft palate).

The lips form the exit of the oral resonator at the free edges of the mouth, and grip, direct and shape the breath stream.

The hard palate is an arched bone structure, separating the oral cavity from the nasal cavities, forming the roof of the mouth.

The soft palate forms the back third of the roof of the mouth, continuing from the curve of the hard palate. The back edge is free and can move up and down. Its movement controls the flow of air through the nose or mouth, like a trap door.

Say the long vowel sound 'ah' with your lower jaw dropped at its most natural point. Continue saying the sound and raise your lower jaw slowly. As the lower jaw comes up, your lips will move closer together and your tongue might move towards the hard palate. You will hear a sound without much oral resonance.

When breathing naturally through the nose, the soft palate is relaxed and relaxes down into the mouth, which leaves the passage to the nose free. When there is an impulse to speak, the soft palate contracts upwards, blocking the passage to the nose, so that the air and sound flows through the mouth.

Breath carries the sound from the pharynx into the mouth. If your breath force is strong enough, the sound will bounce off your hard palate and out through your lips. This is called **forward resonance**. If your breath force is too weak to reach your hard palate, it may pitch onto your soft palate, which will make the sound difficult to project.

Allow your lower jaw to drop at its most natural point and use a mirror to look through to the back of your mouth. If you breathe through your nose and out through your mouth, with your mouth still open, you will see the action of the soft palate.

The mouth is capable of assuming a wide range of sizes and shapes because of the movement of the tongue, lips, jaw and soft palate. However, there needs to be space inside the mouth to create an appropriate amount of oral resonance.

The nose (nasal resonator)

There are two types of nasal resonance:

- when the vibrating column of air passes directly through the open soft palate to the nasal cavity; in English this only happens on three sounds – 'm', 'n' and 'ng'.

- when the vibrating column of air does not pass directly into the nasal cavity, but instead pitches onto the hard palate just behind the upper teeth, and the sound vibrations are carried through the bones of the hard palate to the nasal cavities. This type of nasal resonance can be heard in vowel sounds.

To produce the first type of nasal resonance the soft palate must be in good working order, and to produce the second type of nasal resonance there must be forward resonance (the breath force is strong enough to bounce the sound off the hard palate).

 Say 'mum', 'nose' and 'sing'. Repeat the words but this time hold your nose. You should hear 'bub', 'dose' and 'sig' because there isn't any nasal resonance.

If you have a cold and your nasal cavities are blocked then there won't be any nasal resonance. If your soft palate does not close properly then too much nasal resonance will leak into the sound.

Balancing resonance: Good resonance depends upon achieving a balance of vibration from the pharynx, mouth and nose. The quality of the sound will be affected if there is too much resonance from just one of the resonators.

When you practise your exercises, make sure that your spine is lengthened, your shoulders, neck and jaw are free from tension, and there is space inside your mouth and an adequate breath force to move the sound forward. It is important that you try not to think about all of this theory when you are speaking or performing. You must practise your exercise so that it comes to you naturally.

The quality of sound will also be affected if the resonators are unhealthy (e.g. if you have a cold or sore throat). Unfortunately there is little you can do to counteract the effects of illness on the quality of the sound.

Figure 3: The nose, mouth and pharynx

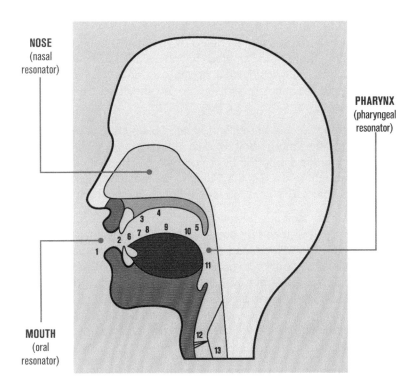

NOSE
(nasal resonator)

PHARYNX
(pharyngeal resonator)

MOUTH
(oral resonator)

1 Lips   2 Teeth   3 Alveolar ridge   4 Hard palate   5 Soft palate
6 Tip of the tongue   7 Blade of the tongue   8 Front of the tongue
9 Centre of the tongue   10 Back of the tongue   11 Root of the tongue
12 Vocal cords or folds   13 Food passage

Head and chest resonance: When you speak, you may also feel vibrations from higher notes in your head and vibrations from lower notes in your chest, which are sometimes called head resonance and chest resonance. However, the head and chest are not official resonators as the vibrations come from sound waves produced by pharyngeal, oral and nasal resonance. For this reason, resonance in the head or chest is sometimes referred to as *secondary resonance*.

Build your projection skills – audibility, audience and space

It is important that you can be heard by your audience in the space where they are assembled. To achieve this, you need more projection than you would use in normal conversation. Due to the flattening out of sounds over distance, you should also use more expression.

With a strong, secure breath and forward placement of resonance a speaker will be more **audible**. A secure breath is released freely and easily and is supported by the correct muscles. Air and sound can be brought forward in the mouth using the hard palate as a sounding board. This is called forward placement of resonance.

The **audience** itself affects your audibility. For example, if your audience is larger than 50 people, you might need a microphone to be audible. If you are faced with loosely spaced people standing in a hall you would have to raise your voice over the head of the person in the front row in order to be heard in the back row. (The solution would be to ask your audience to gather close to you and raise yourself above the audience on a box or stage). A restless audience create sounds of their own that compete with your voice.

The **space** affects your audibility. A big hall can swallow your sound. A building beside a busy road is a bad speaking venue, especially during the commuter rush hour, as is the room beside a restaurant kitchen in the evening. Try to find out from the event organiser what the venue is like before you speak. If there are many elements competing with you, you may be able to make preparations or arrange an alternative space. Otherwise, you will need to use all the projection skills discussed in this chapter to get your message across.

Clarity, diction and fluency

Clarity of speech relies on correct pronunciation and precise articulation of words. A mispronounced word is difficult for an audience to understand and so weakens your message. The phonetic alphabet in the dictionary provides guidance on the correct pronunciation of difficult words.

Good **articulation** relies on using the tongue and lip muscles to form the sound correctly, which requires practice before you have the required muscle memory, so rehearse your speech. If possible, make a recording of it so you can listen to your voice and judge whether your words are clear.

Diction is the choice of words you use and the style with which you enunciate them. To improve your style, tongue-twister exercises can help (refer to chapter *Practice, practice, practice!*).

Fluency is the ability to express oneself easily and relies mostly on not hesitating. Your fluency will improve as you practise your speech. It also improves when you speak at a measured pace rather than trying to speak too fast, because you will have more time to think about what you are going to say next.

Modulation

Modulation is the variation in voice and speech used by the speaker to convey meaning, mood and emotion. This includes varying the use of breath force, pausing, lengthening individual sounds, volume, pace, pitch, inflection, tonal register and intensity. Modulation is especially useful to alert the audience that you have changed to a new topic within your speech. In a **well-modulated** speech you must vary all these elements at the right moments to support your message and help your audience to understand it.

(a) **Emphasis** is when a speaker attaches extra prominence to a particular word or thought by using modulation. For example, dramatic emphasis can be achieved by increasing the intensity of the breath force, building volume and widening the pitch range.

If there is **underemphasis**, speech becomes dull, flat and monotonous. Sometimes, in certain types of humour, it can be used effectively, but this should be thought of as a technique rather than the normal means of communication.

If there is **overemphasis**, speech can become irritating and tiring to listen to.

Sometimes, stressing one word can affect its meaning in the sentence. For example:

- Did she give you the book? No, *he* gave me the book.
- Did you steal the book? No, he *gave* me the book.
- Is the book hers? No, he gave *me* the book.
- Did he give you the pen? No, he gave me the *book*.

To achieve extra emphasis, lengthen the individual sounds in the word, as in: 'How will we achieve this? <u>Ed-u-cation</u>.'

To keep your speech clear and lively, stress the important words that convey information or opinion in your sentences and soften the unimportant words.

(b) A **pause** is when sound stops. Pausing is a particularly useful technique for speaking in public. You need deeper breaths for public speaking to support your voice projection, and you cannot breathe while talking. Therefore, you need pauses.

A pause for emphasis may be made before a word or phrase, after the word or phrase, or, for extra strong emphasis, both before and after the word or phrase. The word or phrase is, therefore, isolated and achieves prominence. Carefully timed, a pause will build suspense and climax, but holding a pause for too long will break the spell.

Observe how effective an **emphatic pause** is in this example, when you are informed by the speaker that their story was not believed by the fishermen of Lofoden and again when you realise that the story is to be told to you:

> I told them my story—they did not believe it. I now tell it to you—and I can scarcely expect you to put more faith in it than did the merry fishermen of Lofoden.
>
> Edgar Allan Poe (1809–1849),
> *A Descent Into The Maelström*

In an **emotional pause** the voice is suspended by the strong working of the emotions. It must be used with great subtlety or it will sound over-dramatic and insincere. In this sentence from *Jane Eyre* by Charlotte Brontë (1816–1855), there are two emotional pauses to convey the character's emotions when speaking:

> 'Wicked and cruel boy!' I said. 'You are like a murderer—you are like a slave-driver—you are like the Roman emperors!'

(c) **Volume** is the level of loudness or softness with which you speak. You should vary your volume to create a well-modulated delivery but for most speeches you need only the gentlest crescendo (becoming louder) and diminuendo (becoming softer). If you use too much breath force then you will shout. Shouting lacks subtlety and can make your audience uncomfortable.

(d) **Pace** is the rate at which you speak (words per minute). Change your pace to convey your meaning and mood.

A **slower pace** can be achieved by lengthening sounds and lengthening the space between words. Words suggesting size, effort, astonishment and long periods of time can be taken more slowly. Using an exotic word instead of a simple one slows your talk as the audience pauses to ponder its meaning. Emotional passages tend to be taken at a slower pace. A phrase which contains several ideas might be taken more slowly and deliberately than one with a simple idea. Using many short sentences can sometimes slow the pace down.

A **faster pace** can be achieved by shortening sounds and shortening the space between words. Quick, easy, ordinary things can be spoken about more rapidly. An increase in pace can also be used to build to a climax. Pace is affected by the distribution of stresses in a phrase. Lighter stressing and a more rhythmical distribution of stresses can be taken at a swifter pace. A simple way to increase the pace is to link every sentence with a connecting word: but, and, however.

Most beginners tend to speak too quickly and can benefit from a slower pace.

(e) **Pitch** is the specific level of highness or lowness in a speech note. A higher pitch is often used for lighter and happier thoughts. A lower pitch is often used for sombre and sad thoughts. Vary your pitch to avoid sounding monotonous and to support the mood you wish to create.

(f) **Inflection** is the rise and fall in the pitch of your voice during speech. As your voice rises and falls it forms patterns or tunes. Inflection reflects your personality, your thoughts and your feelings. Flexible use of inflection will, therefore, reveal subtle changes in your moods, but it should not require conscious effort or your speech can become stilted. Take special care of your inflection at the ends of sentences. Use variety to keep your audience engaged and to release emotion.

Falling tune is a simple falling pattern where the stressed syllables descend from a higher pitch to a lower one, as in 'Put that on the table.' It tends to be used for completing statements, commands, agreement, aggression and strong emotion.

Rising tune is a pattern of descending stressed syllables, but there is a rise of pitch on the last syllable, as in 'Would you like to come to the football match?' It tends to be used for doubt, anxiety, surprise, pleading and questions requiring a 'yes' or 'no' answer.

(g) **Tonal register**, or timbre, refers to the variation of 'light' and 'shade' in your voice. Although your voice box will dictate the overall tone of your voice, you can speak the same word at the same pitch but with a different tone. In a similar way to inflection, the speaker's emotions affect the tonal register, and that helps the listener to recognise the mood of the speaker, regardless of the words spoken. The simplest way to match your tonal register to your audience, purpose and situation is to identify appropriate emotions that you want to project and mark them in the left margin of your speech notes. Your voice will adjust automatically once you have the emotion in mind. You should change the emotions used in your speech to maintain interest. Really? (he said, timidly). Really! (he said, with certainty).

(h) **Intensity:** Changes in modulation can create tension or relaxation. A speaker should avoid giving a whole speech at high intensity (for instance, strong emphasis, raised volume, fast pace and an impassioned tone) because it can be too tiring for both the speaker and audience. The value of contrast and sincerity would be lost. If you whip your audience into a frenzy of excitement, you must allow them time to calm down and reflect on what you have said.

Engaging your audience

You must try to engage the audience right from the start and keep their attention throughout the speech. To achieve this you must be sincere and **enthusiastic**. This will be easy if you believe in what you are saying and are pleased to be saying it. That is why it is so important to base your speech on a subject that is both interesting to the audience and that you are passionate about.

Rather than worrying about your nervousness, think instead of how you can help your audience by presenting your speech well. Your listeners will detect your interest and this will improve their attitude and their belief in what you say.

You can copy techniques that work for other speakers – but do not try to mimic their personality. The more you try to 'put on' a personality the more artificial you will appear. What you have to *say* should be the most interesting part of your speech – try to develop a relaxed manner, which allows your personality to be natural.

You can also engage the audience through **variety**. Alternate between stories, facts, quotes, analysis, ideas and various visual aids (if appropriate) – all this helps to make your speech fresh and engaging. A mix of long and short sentences in your speech makes it interesting and encourages you to change your pitch and pace, which keeps the audience stimulated.

Spontaneity

Beware of knowing your speech so well that you can deliver it automatically, or of being so under-rehearsed that you need to read every word. In both cases you will not be mentally engaged and your speech will lack spontaneity. A well-delivered speech sounds as if it is being presented for the very first time, but it has been rehearsed and prepared. Spontaneity comes from a combination of knowledge of the content, modulation, sincerity and enthusiasm.

Pause occasionally, re-energise and say the next line as if it is a totally new idea that has just occurred to you. Allow yourself to be excited about the moment of delivery – it will help you to think on your feet and respond to unexpected challenges.

Audibility

You may have a prize-winning speech but it is useless if your audience is unable to hear you. Speak up! Do not slur your words or use slang substitutes, because your message will be lost. If you are using a microphone and you mumble, it will simply amplify the mumble; it will not change your speech from a mumble into clear diction. Be sure that you form the words clearly and that you do not rush through your speech.

Rehearse your delivery to practise the modulation techniques you have learned, and find the level your voice needs to project well. Practise changes in your voice to adapt to whatever circumstances you have to speak in. Whether you use a microphone or not, you must not shout at your audience because this will disengage them and make you seem arrogant. Use a warm and friendly tone that is easy to listen to, but conveys your confidence in your knowledge.

Mental engagement

You engage your audience mentally when you stimulate them to think about what you are saying. This can involve everything that you do – for example, the words you use; the content of your speech; your posture; how you deliver your speech; and whether you have good eye contact with audience members. When you focus your attention on your audience (and not on yourself) you enhance your speech through mental projection. This does not mean that your audience magically receives your thoughts. It means that because you are trying to extend your presence to the far corners of the space, you automatically begin to raise your voice to a suitable level, you notice the puzzled expressions of the people on the right who can't see your visual aid – and you become aware that the people on the back row are sleeping and need a question to wake them up!

Mental projection helps you to engage the audience. Have no fear – they will never know how nervous you are or the mistakes you think you have made. **Fear means you are thinking of yourself – think of the audience!** What can you do to help them understand?

Do not underestimate your audience by assuming that they will not understand complicated ideas. If you over-simplify your speech, they will feel patronised. If you try to impress them by using ornate words and phrases they may think you are self-important. Try to find the balance, which relies on relevant words that get your message across to the kind of people sitting in your audience. Be sure that you understand every word that you say, so you can sound sincere.

Speak *to* them, not *at* them. If you are too forceful, the audience will react negatively to what you say. Aim to **share** your work with your audience, rather than merely transmitting the information.

Quick thinking

If problems arise which your audience do not need to know about (you have lost your notes), pretend to be confident and in control. If problems arise during your speech (the builders begin using the drill next door) do not ignore the problem – ask the management of the event to resolve it, or deal with it yourself so you can return to your speech without further interruptions. Your audience will appreciate your concern for their comfort.

If you are running out of time, skip past one of your points in your talk and cut out supporting material like stories and further facts. As long as you mention your most important points and present your strong conclusion with your call to take action, you can be confident you have done your job.

Sometimes you need to improvise. See chapter *Practice, practice, practice!* for games that will help develop your ability for quick thinking. The more prepared you are, the less you will have to rely on quick thinking to get you out of a corner. You could prepare your answers to the most likely questions, and have an extra story ready that illustrates one of your points in case you have to speak for longer than you thought.

Being confronted by a hostile crowd that fires **awkward questions** is the realm of the politician. Although it is a common fear for speakers, it is unlikely that you will need to field questions during your speech, unless you invite them. Most audiences have chosen to be there because they are interested in the topic you are presenting, so they will give you the chance to show them what you have prepared. The more engaging your speech, the more supportive they will become.

You can simply delay answering questions by explaining that you will reply at the end of your talk, unless you feel that the question is shared by all members of the audience and will make a big difference in convincing them of your point of view. To buy yourself time to think, you can repeat the question out loud for the benefit of those who might not have heard it clearly. You can also ask a question of your own to seek clarification: 'To help me answer that, can you tell me why you are asking that question? What are you trying to find out?'

Be confident

Good preparation builds your confidence, because your research gives you a good command of the subject, so you will not be nervous about questions. Good organisation helps to develop confidence because it allows you to focus on your speech without last-minute complications. Finally, good posture will build your confidence because it helps you to breathe well and enhance your speech; so stand tall and relax your shoulders. It is most important to *appear* confident, even if you don't feel that way. Paradoxically, the more confident you appear, the more confident you will become.

A simple technique to appear more confident is to eliminate your filler words like 'er', 'um' and 'ah' and to use a pause in their place. These filler words are useful in two-way conversations to give you a moment to collect your thoughts and to indicate that you haven't finished speaking yet, to prevent someone else cutting in. However, when you are presenting or speaking in public, the audience expect you to continue talking. They will wait without speaking. The extra pause allows them to consider your words, and can improve the measured pace of your delivery.

To get started, practise removing your filler words from your everyday conversations.

Reducing nerves

It is natural to be nervous. The secret is to stop your nervousness building so much that it controls you. Nervousness can produce positive energy for the delivery of your speech – it makes you feel alive, alert and aware. Control your nerves by:

- taking slow, deep breaths
- thinking of the audience as friends and not enemies
- believing in the subject you are going to share.

Some people want everything they do to be perfect. It is good to strive for excellence, but perfectionism could make you nervous (because you know you will make at least one little mistake, somewhere) and have a negative impact on your speech. No speech is perfect; everything can be improved. Focus on delivering a better speech than your last one, by *improving* rather than by being perfect.

Eye contact

When you look at a listener, you make them feel noticed and important, so they naturally return the favour by noticing what you are saying. This non-verbal communication is an essential part of your delivery.

Make eye contact with your audience at the beginning of your speech (and that includes the Examiner during a LAMDA Examination). Smile – this will help you to engage the audience and will make you feel more relaxed. Take in the whole audience with a sweeping glance; then sustain eye contact throughout the talk by focusing on different sections of the audience equally. Do not stare at one person, and avoid staring at the ceiling, the floor, or one particular spot at the back of the room. Find a new face in each section of the audience on every pass and imagine that you are speaking only to them, for a few seconds.

When people talk to each other in conversation, there is a powerful incentive to pay attention – they might at any time be asked a question and be expected to respond. When you are sitting in an audience, however, you can 'switch off' because you are not expected to respond. But if the speaker looks at you directly, it makes you feel as if you might suddenly be asked a question. This makes you pay attention and thus makes the speech more effective. Trigger this response in your audience by continually making eye contact.

Body language

A speaker talking about trust and honesty should stand still because that suggests calmness and authority. However, for a talk on fitness, such a calm stance might seem too passive – to support that subject you need to display vitality with some movement.

Your **gestures** can support and emphasise points in your speech. Beware of over-planning gestures and making them mechanical and unnatural. Your gestures communicate your individuality. Allow your gestures to arise naturally from what you are saying.

Try to avoid repeating gestures too often. The audience might start counting how many times you have used a certain movement – when this happens they have stopped paying attention to what you are saying and are more involved in what you are doing because you have ceased to engage them.

Other habits that can distract audiences are fiddling with jewellery and items of clothing. Avoid putting your hands in your pockets and rattling keys or loose change. If you wear glasses, do not allow them to become a source of distraction by taking them on and off when it is unnecessary.

If your speech does not require any movement or reference to visual aids, then keep still and do not move from your neutral stance (poised and relaxed, rather than standing rigidly to attention).

Body language can emphasise what you say, as long as it is relevant and arises naturally from what you are saying and how you feel. You can **use your face** to add visible emotion to intense moments in your speech. For instance, if you are describing a scenario where you were threatened, you may want to take an aggressive stance and add an intense gaze and expression. Use this technique sparingly.

Some speeches require movement. If you are using a microphone ensure that it is mobile too.

Use the available space to enhance your speech. If you sit close to your audience, you create an intimate mood, which would match a speech where the information you're sharing is confidential. Standing is usually a posture that allows you to use your voice well and suits most topics, which benefit from bold presentation.

Standing in the centre of the space makes you seem more commanding; standing close makes you intimidating or oppressive; standing against the wall is unconventional, but might suit a speech about being bullied at school because it shows that you do not feel confident at all.

Stepping on stage

Your **entrance** will leave a strong impression. When the chairperson introduces you, your heart may begin to beat faster – you can relax by taking some deep breaths (see chapter *Practice, practice, practice!*). Use this time to look at the audience. Think of them as being 'on your side' and find one friendly face to address at the start of your speech. This will make it easier to begin with confidence.

Once you have been introduced, get up naturally and move to the podium with a sense of purpose. Acknowledge the chairperson with a thank you or a handshake. Pause. Before you speak, be sure that the microphone is in the right position and that you don't have to lean forward in an unnatural manner to speak into it. Place your notes or note cards where you can see them. This may seem to cause a long delay, but it will only be seconds, and it will ensure that when you begin to speak you are comfortable and the audience can hear you clearly. It will also give you a moment to adjust to the situation and gain composure.

If you have been told to speak at a lectern, do not clutch it on either side as if your life depended on it. This will cause tension, which will affect your voice. Better to keep your hands by your sides most of the time. (However, gripping the lectern could occasionally be employed for real impact in a message.) If the point of delivery is a table, do not be tempted to stoop forward to read your notes or note cards – pick them up. You cannot engage your audience with the top of your head – they need to see your face and hear your voice.

A solid performance

This begins with your preparation and ends with engaging the audience with a confident and sincere delivery.

Limit your choice to those subjects of which you have special knowledge or make sure that your research is thorough, so you can speak with authority. A good knowledge of the subject, combined with good preparation, is vital. This begins with the details you obtain when the booking is made and continues with the research of your subject, the arrangement of your material, transferring this into note form, deciding whether or not to use visual aids and practising with them, and preparing your voice, speech and personal appearance.

Arrive early to check everything at the venue. Leave nothing to chance that can cause you to panic. Finally, believe in what you say and speak it clearly, unhurriedly and with enthusiasm and sincerity. When you step on to the stage, it is yours for the duration of the speech, so act as if you own the space, the story and the attention of the audience. Enjoy the opportunity.

Holding a conversation

Sometimes participating in conversation can be difficult. You may be afraid of sounding ill-prepared or rude, or speaking out of turn. The most important thing to learn is to listen. Listening can give you clues to know when to speak.

If you are asked a question like: 'What is your favourite music?' you could answer: 'I like pop music! What is your favourite kind?' The **follow-up question** is relevant to the subject and the situation. Answering the question politely and then following it with a relevant question initiates a reply. This kind of turn taking can continue as long as the speakers continue to add a different question after their response.

Tagging an irrelevant question on to the end of a conversation is not enough. You must be involved in what is being discussed and display this with relevant questions and an appropriate expression. You can always use friendly and enthusiastic questions to continue the conversation, but be polite and use words that suit the occasion. Lead the other person into talking about what *they* did, or what *they* like, or what *they* think. The key to a good conversation is not in talking about yourself, but in asking questions about the other person.

Based on your understanding of what someone has told you, you can also **initiate an idea of your own**. For example, if they were talking about how many small birds have not survived the cold winter you could mention how you saw a sparrow fall out of a tree. However, it must relate to what has been said or it will seem you have not been listening at all. Do not tell them about the pet sparrow you once owned – although it is a bird, it is not a bird that was affected by the cold of the winter.

If there is a question-and-answer session after your speech it is important that you **listen carefully** to the questions in order to be able to respond appropriately. This is part of your communication of your subject and an opportunity for you to underline what you have said in your speech to support the ideas you have expressed.

If you do not understand a question, ask for it to be repeated or explained. If you have an awkward, or even ambiguous, question you can clarify this by saying something like: 'Am I right in thinking that you mean…?' This will give you time to think of your reply.

Whatever your subject, be certain of your facts so that you can deal with questions confidently. When answering questions always be honest. Lack of knowledge and authority will be exposed if someone challenges a statement you have made. Therefore, choose a subject you really know about.

While you are speaking, it is important to maintain your **awareness of the audience**. To do this, keep regular eye contact with different audience members. Position your notes so that you do not have to look far away from the audience when scanning for your next point. This is why a lectern is the shape it is, with your notes raised just below your eyeline and angled so that you can easily see them. For a similar reason, do not try to hide your note cards against your body, because you will need to crane your neck every time you check for a cue. When you need to look at your cards, raise them to a comfortable position at chest height.

In one-to-one conversation, don't stare into the other person's eyes without looking away briefly and regularly, but keep bringing your gaze back to their face. This makes you seem interested in what they are saying because you seem to be watching their expression for clues to what they feel about the topic.

If you are using a visual aid, point to it, turn to the audience again, and then talk about it. Presenters often face their projected PowerPoint slides for too long, while they read off all the points and elaborate on them. The audience needs to see your face to read important visual clues.

If you are part of a team (for example, a chairperson, a speaker and someone giving a vote of thanks), you will be required to participate. To keep your focus and **concentration** you must really listen to what the other speakers are saying. Listen as though you are in a conversation and are expected to respond with an answer. A good public speaker knows when to be silent and to listen and learn, as well as when to speak.

If you have chosen a non-controversial subject to speak on, you can relax because you are not as likely to have many contentious questions. If you are nervous about the kind of questions you may be asked, or worried that there may not even be *any* questions, there are several ways of dealing with this:

- Prepare some questions yourself and plant them in the audience with reliable friends or committee members (they will ask these questions when you call for them).
- Have a member of the organising committee solicit questions before the meeting and refer to these.
- Suggest the question to the audience yourself, by saying 'What can be done about...?' and following it up with the answer.

If you choose to leave it to the audience, then listen carefully. You may, if you wish to do so, increase continuation of the conversation by listening carefully to the style of questions being asked, and from this, assess the mood and thoughts of the group to direct further discussion.

In any gathering there will be people who are not afraid to speak up and share in the debate and others who are intimidated by the situation. You can **create opportunities** for them to contribute. Try to draw these quiet ones into the conversation. An example of how this could be done would be to say to the last speaker: 'That's a very good point,' then looking directly at someone you wish to encourage: 'I wonder what *you* think about this? Do you agree?' If you wish to make it a more general drawing in of any members of the group, you could encourage anyone to speak up with: 'Does anyone else have something to say about this?'

If you are the chairperson or a member of the platform party and someone else is delivering a speech, be sure to **support** them. This will help to create attentiveness among the audience, if they become aware of your non-verbal support. Listen to every word that is said and look at the speaker, nodding gently in agreement when they make a point and reacting positively with a thoughtful facial expression. Be sure that this is genuine and not overdone. Otherwise you will upstage the speaker and distract the audience. This kind of non-verbal support is encouraging to the speaker, especially if you are sitting in the audience.

If your role is, for example, to propose a vote of thanks, provide the summary speech in a debate or give the closing speech after a panel discussion, you must listen attentively to the speaker(s) and **make notes of the key points**. In a well-constructed and well-delivered speech, these will be easy to recognise. However, in a speech that lacks structure, it is your job to listen well and find the main points. Take the title as your yardstick and relate your points to this, so you can follow the reasoning. Make your notes and then choose one point from them to reiterate in your vote of thanks, relating it to its importance to this particular gathering. For example, if the speech was entitled 'Travelling with confidence', you could say: 'It was of great interest to us all to hear about the currency requirements in some of the countries that our group will be visiting next year. We will certainly plan with this in mind...' This kind of reference to a specific point is encouraging to the speaker. It will show the speaker that the audience have paid attention.

Support material

The use of support material, such as visual aids, can allow you to increase your **contact** with the audience.

Visual aids

Visual aids can take many forms (for example: books, exhibits, flip charts, posters and projected images). Although not always essential, they often provide good support material for a speech by highlighting key points in a unique way. They can attract attention, stimulate interest and make your meaning clear. People like to be shown things that help them to understand what a speaker is talking about. The best type of visual aid will depend a great deal on your subject.

If you are addressing a small group you may want to use **illustrations** from a book. You must practise handling it to save yourself the embarrassment of fumbling or dropping it. To avoid this, you could photocopy and enlarge the illustrations and attach them to a card, which could be easily displayed.

If you have visual aids, make reference to them during your speech. It is frustrating for an audience to see interesting visual aids laid out but never referred to. They will wonder what they are there for. Practise using them in the correct way: touch or point to the visual, turn to face the audience again, then talk. If they are static, move towards them. Always pause for the audience to absorb the pictorial information.

Visual aids are a form of non-verbal emphasis. Overuse of visual aids, has the same result as overuse of emphasis; if you emphasise everything, nothing is emphasised. Use visual aids economically and wisely.

Finally, be certain that the visual aids you have chosen are **suitable** for the audience.

Visual aids should be chosen with the size of the venue and the audience in mind and should, therefore, be **large enough** for everyone in the room or the auditorium to see. Do not alienate members of your audience sitting at the back or the sides by having visual aids that are only clearly visible from the first few rows; and do not alienate the whole of your audience by using visual aids that are too small for anyone to see.

This also applies to visual aids that have **too much information** on them. Visual aids can help to represent complex information graphically, but they must be simple enough to understand. The best way to share detailed information is via a **handout** or link to a **website** (to be read after your speech).

A **flip chart** allows you to draw simple diagrams and write key words, which reinforce what you are explaining to your audience. If you draw as you go along, the information is presented at a slow pace that helps the audience to absorb it. Charts can be prepared earlier with relevant material to turn over and display at the correct moment in your speech, but be careful of presenting an overwhelming amount of information. If you are addressing the type of meeting where involving the audience would help you to make your point, you could use a flip chart to write down the ideas offered by members of the audience. This can help you to appear spontaneous and lively, but it can be challenging for beginners in public speaking to manage the flip chart well, so it needs practice.

Posters can help to illustrate particular aspects of a talk and can be displayed easily. Just be sure to check that a display stand or board is available at the venue.

A projector can help to gain your audience's interest and, if used wisely, can illustrate your speech well. It ensures visual clarity if the screen is correctly placed. But using too many images can distract the audience from the subject matter and lose the impact that you want. PowerPoint is a common software program used to prepare and present digital slides. If you use PowerPoint be sure that each slide is relevant, and that it clarifies or illuminates what you are saying. If you removed the slide, would your audience still get your message? Be especially careful of PowerPoint pages crammed with words: use very few, if any, words. It is a *visual* aid, not a projection of your notes. If the slide is detailed, allow the audience time to understand what the various elements represent (the axes of the graph, the colours and the shapes) before discussing what it proves. Start and finish on a blank slide to bring their attention back to you, the speaker.

If you choose to use any form of technical support material, test it first and be prepared for it to fail. Whatever support material you use, be sure to use it efficiently and in a **relevant** manner: in other words, ensure that the images have a direct link to your topic and are ones the audience can relate to. The most effective visual aids are those that support your subject matter.

Timing is very important. If you are giving a talk on children's charities and wish to alert your audience to the effects of flooding, you should not place pictures of homeless, starving children all over the stage. This would destroy the impact you wish to make. Wait for an appropriate point in your speech and then reveal one visual aid and follow it by another. Your words combined with the visual impact will be an effective motivation to your audience to want to do something about it.

Your notes

Your notes are your personal support materials. In most situations, your words should not be read out. Reading from a full-length written speech inhibits your spontaneity and makes you rush. When you have prepared your speech and structured your information, mark key points. Practise the speech a few times, and when you have become familiar with your material, transfer these key points onto note cards, as mentioned in chapter *Planning and preparation*. These will be your memory aids as you speak and will help to keep you on the right track. Refer to them by briefly glancing down, picking one clear phrase at a time.

It is more important to **know your subject** than to know your *speech*. If you know your subject, the memory notes will be all you need to keep the structure and order of your speech. The advantage of using cards is that they will not rustle when you turn them over and they will not blow away if there is a sudden draught. You will also be able to handle cards more easily. A comfortable size is 10 centimetres by 15. Write on one side only, so your audience are not distracted by trying to read what is on the back of your cards. Number the cards clearly to prevent mixing them up, or join them together with a tag through one corner so that you can easily flip them from front to back.

Use notes in an **appropriate** way. If you begin your speech by saying 'Hello, I am Cally Clutterbox,' then look down at your notes and say 'I am the Assistant Chief Stationery Coordinator and have been working at Officers' Offices for eight years' (because that is what you wrote on your note card), your audience will begin to wonder if you are lying (you have been there eight years and cannot remember your own job title?). Rather, write 'who I am in the company, what I do' and leave it to your powers of memory to supply the information as you speak. Beware of resting your gaze on your notes – your gaze should bounce off your notes and return to the audience as soon as you have seen your next point.

When you ask the audience prepared questions (rhetorical or otherwise) you must look directly at the audience and not at your cards. Scan the card first, look up, pause, then ask your question.

If you have an important and lengthy quote, a technical definition or scientific research figures that require precision, it is appropriate to read these from the card if you cannot remember them, but be sure to look up regularly to maintain eye contact. Make this look like a deliberate part of the speech.

Microphones

If you are speaking in a large hall and you are provided with a microphone, it is advisable to use it to avoid straining your voice. Here are several points to remember.

Microphones are directional. Many microphones will only amplify your voice if you speak directly into them. If your microphone is fixed and you move your head to engage with the whole audience, the volume will be variable as your voice comes and goes; this is distracting to the audience. In these cases it is better to use a 'clip mike' or, if this is not possible, to hold the microphone in your hand.

Microphones are sensitive. You will have to control your volume because you can cause a feedback screech. If you become too animated or begin to fiddle with your notes or any other item, the microphone will amplify all of this, including any asides you may make to the chairperson. Check the sensitivity of the microphone you are using when you do your venue preparation.

Microphones are useful. Even a well-trained voice can benefit from the use of a microphone. Learn to use it well and you may even come to regard it as a friend.

Beware of speaking too closely to the bare microphone. If it does not have a foam sock on, then hold it at least a couple of inches away from your mouth to avoid rebound, particularly from plosive consonants such as /p/ and /b/. Practise with a microphone whenever possible.

If you are not speaking clearly, a microphone will amplify your lack of clarity. Speak clearly into the microphone and it will carry your message clearly to the corners of the room.

Microphones are not permitted for use in LAMDA Examinations.

Practice, practice, practice!

Your presentation skills will improve with practise. Take any opportunity you can to present subjects to an audience. The more you practise, the more confident you will become. If you are preparing for a speech, rehearse your performance out loud from beginning to end without stopping or going back on yourself. Speak in front of a mirror, with a voice recorder (or even better, video recorder) if you have one. Some friends can help by being an audience and giving you feedback. Do at least one full technical rehearsal using all your visual aids and the equipment you will be expected to use.

This chapter contains exercises to develop specific speaking skills. It includes breathing exercises, voice-work exercises and games to improve your abilities in various situations. Regular use of these breathing techniques and speech exercises will improve your communication.

Relax

Stand with your feet shoulder-width apart. Stretch up, with your arms as high as possible and your fingers extended. Slowly flop down from the waist, with your upper body hanging limply over your feet. Let your arms swing loose. Then, gradually grow back into the upright position with your head coming up last and your shoulders relaxed. Shake out.

Breathe

Because you have to breathe to stay alive, it is easy to think that you know all about breathing. In fact, more breath and more control is needed when you speak; particularly when you speak in public. To develop good breath support, you should breathe 'from your stomach' (drawing the breath down deeply) without raising your shoulders.

Try these exercises to develop breath control:

a) Take a deep breath and blow an imaginary feather gently for as long as you can.

b) You've just turned 100. Blow out all the candles on your imaginary birthday cake.

c) Imagine that there is a balloon just above your face and you have to keep it balanced in the same position by blowing gently. Not too hard, as this would blow the balloon away, but not so gently that the balloon would touch your face. This exercise helps you to extend your breaths, but also to control the amount of air you are using at any one time.

Concentrate on the activity of your ribs, rib muscles and diaphragm and learn to use the whole chest area and fill your lungs with air to support your voice. When you breathe in to speak, the intercostal muscles are the first to start moving. They move the ribs outwards and upwards, and as this movement begins the diaphragm starts to move downwards and flattens. This movement creates a cavity for the lungs to fill with air. The air rushes in to equalise the pressure and the abdominal muscles relax.

When you use the breath to speak, the reverse action happens. The abdominal muscles help to control the diaphragm as it returns to its dome shape and the ribs relax to their natural position. This control can help you to project your voice in large halls and also reach the end of long phrases.

To identify these muscles and learn to use them, lie down with your head supported slightly with a small pillow or a book. Because you are lying down you can concentrate completely on the chest area and your breathing without having to support your spine, legs or any other part of your body.

Place one hand on your ribs and one hand on the area just below the chest and above the waist or navel. Breathe in, first of all being aware of the movement of the ribs being pulled outwards and upwards by the intercostal muscles, then immediately followed by the movement of the diaphragm downwards, which will make the upper middle part of the abdomen swell. You have now created a cavity, which is filled immediately with air.

Once you have correctly identified this activity you can train the muscles to react to you and build your breath control and capacity by doing exercises (still lying on the floor).

Do not rush this process. Allow the muscles to become familiar and responsive before you move on to the next stage.

(a) Breathe in slowly for a count of three and then out for a count of three.

(b) Breathe in for a count of three, hold it for a count of three and breathe out for a count of three.

(c) Increase the count slowly to seven.

(d) Use a drinking straw and blow gently through it to keep a real balloon steady in the air above you.

(e) Use a drinking straw to pick up peas and carry them on the end of the straw to the other side of the room, held in position only by your breath. Extend the time you hold the pea.

Resonate

When your breath has travelled through your vocal cords and created voice, it then echoes in the vocal cavities of your head. These resonators amplify the voice, and using them can help you to increase your area of delivery.

Standing with your feet slightly apart and your shoulders relaxed, breathe in and then let the air out on a hum. This makes the cavity of the nose work. Do this several times.

Now, when you have begun to hum, gradually open your mouth on an /aː/ or /ah/ sound. So you have very slowly said the word 'mar': *Mmmmaaaaaaaaaar*. Keep the sound going to the end of the breath. Be sure to open your mouth wide by dropping your jaw.

Practise this several times and listen to hear how much the sound improves as you become more confident in what you are doing. This is because by beginning with a hum and making the cavity of the nose work and then opening your mouth wide on the /aː/ sound, all the head cavities – the nose, the pharynx, the mouth and the sinus cavities – are working together. This will help your voice carry across a large space.

Work to make the jaw more flexible by looking in the mirror and opening your mouth as wide as you can. Then allow the jaw to drop in a relaxed way; then close it. Practise opening and closing your mouth like this several times.

When you have done this, repeat the long hum followed by the '*mar*' /maː/ sound, each time trying to improve the clarity and increase the length of the note and the breath.

Speak clearly

A mirror is a good tool to help you practise these sounds and to watch what is happening to your mouth as you make them. This will increase your awareness when you speak and help you to remember to speak with precision.

Look in the mirror and push your lips forward to form a /w/. Pull your lips back and exaggerate the movement. Repeat.

Stick your tongue out at yourself. Now try to reach your nose with your tongue tip, then your chin, then your left ear and then your right ear. These tongue exercises will help with flexibility and firmness of speech.

The jaw exercises given for resonance can be used effectively for a weak /r/ sound. This can be combined with attention to the position of the lips, which should never be formed into a /w/ position when making a /r/, but kept relaxed and spread.

Look in the mirror, beginning with your lips firmly closed, and make a /p/ sound by forcing the air through to make an explosion. Do this again, but this time add voice to make a /b/.

Practise a succession of *p p p p p* then *b b b b b*.

In the same manner, place your tongue just behind your top teeth and make a /t/ sound followed by a /d/. Practise a succession of *t t t t t* then *d d d d d*.

Combine these sounds in words and repeat: *bibberty babberty, bibberty babberty, bibberty babberty* and *pitter patter, pitter patter, pitter patter*. Repeat these sounds as often as you can.

Make a /k/ and then a /g/ sound and feel where they are made as you make them. Be aware of the contact made by the back of the tongue and the soft palate. Practise a succession of *k k k k k* and *g g g g g*. Follow this by *kicker, kicker, kicker, kicker, kicker* and *gigger, gigger, gigger, gigger, gigger*.

Place your lower lip and upper teeth together and push the air through to make /f/ and /v/ sounds. Continue the flow of air with your lip and teeth still in contact to make a continuous *fffff* and *vvvvv*.

Place your tongue tip and upper teeth together to make the sound that the letters 'th' form.

Thththththth. First do this quietly on the breath as in the word 'thing'. Then do it with voice added as in the word 'this'. Finally say *this thing, this thing, this thing, this thing, this thing*.

Look in the mirror and place your lips in a tiny circle to make the sound /u:/ or /oo/. Now open your mouth more to make the short sound /o/ as in /off/. Then begin with a short /o/ and glide to /oo/ and you have made an /au:/ sound. Practise: *oo aw ah er ay ee*.

Now put some of the consonants with them and combine the sounds:

poo paw pah, poo paw pah, poo paw pah, poo paw pah

too taw tah, too taw tah, too taw tah, too taw tah

toot toot tawt tawt poop poop pawp pawp

Any sequence of consonants and vowels can be used to encourage clarity and flexibility.

Beware of intrusive consonants. This means consonants that are often wrongly added between words, when one word finishes on a vowel sound and the other word begins with a vowel sound. So 'law and order' becomes 'law rand order'. To avoid this be sure you complete the /aw/ sound before you begin the /and/. Always be sure when you are using two vowels together in this way that you finish the first sound before you begin the next one.

Just a minute

This warm-up game works best with a partner or a group. Speak on a given topic for one minute, without hesitation, repetition or deviation. Topics can be diverse or unusual. Once you have begun, others in the group interrupt via the chairperson, who times the speakers. If the reason behind the interruption is justified, then they continue with the speech and have the remaining time to finish.

Persuade me

Take an ordinary object such as a pen, tie or t-shirt. Imagine that you are a market stall holder and improvise a short speech trying to persuade your audience that your product is very special and everyone should buy it. This exercise requires two or more people. After everyone has presented their speech, discuss the effectiveness of each speech and say which one you found to be the most persuasive.

Pitch

This exercise can be done on your own or with other people.

Pitch:

(a) a suit that shrinks the wearer down two sizes

(b) a chocolate bar that increases the eater's ability to memorise facts

(c) a pen that enables the writer to spell every word correctly.

Now, thinking about the sales pitches that you have just made, would your pitch differ depending on what types of people your audience were made of? Imagine the same pitch in front of an audience which may include:

(a) a group of peers

(b) a group of financiers, who may be persuaded to back the invention

(c) members of the target market for the product.

Discuss the effectiveness of each mini-speech, looking at differences in vocal pitch, vocabulary, manner and attitude.

Research

Select a key character from history whom you believe has made a difference to society. Research details about the key character (or, if in a workshop setting, the main facts could be listed on note cards that are handed out). Prepare a short speech to persuade your audience (while pretending to be the key character) that you should either gain the last place:

(a) as a sculpture in an important city square,

or

(b) in a spaceship flying away from doomed Earth.

Be appropriate

Prepare a one-minute speech of welcome and a short vote of thanks for one of the following people who are visiting your college:

(a) a fellow student who has just won the lottery

(b) a pop star, actor or writer of your choice

(c) a member of the Royal Family.

If you are working with more than one person, discuss the speeches with them. Try to identify appropriate and inappropriate words.

Project your voice

Stand far away from your partner and imagine you are in a crowded room. Begin a conversation with your partner. Raise or lower your hand to indicate the volume you can hear.

Continue the conversation as you walk towards each other, imagining that you are pushing your way through the crowded room. As you get nearer, your voice should become softer and your conversation more detailed. You suddenly realise you are late for an appointment...continue the conversation as you separate.

Change your tone

Pretend you are a teacher and your partner is your student. Change the way your response sounds according to the description in brackets.

Student: I was late because... [add reason]
Teacher: Oh. (calm acceptance of reason)
Student: I was late because... [add reason]
Teacher: Oh? (questioning)
Student: I was late because... [add reason]
Teacher: Oh! (disbelieving)
Student: I was late because... [add reason]
Teacher: Oh! (furious)
Student: I was late because... [add reason]
Teacher: Oh! (amused)
Student: I was late because... [add reason]
Teacher: Oh. (disappointed)

Take note

This works best with a large group. Each member tells their favourite story to a listener, who makes notes, concentrating on a brief but accurate recall of key characters, key incidents and the main storyline. The listeners move on to a different person, to whom they retell the story. The exercise continues, with partners constantly changing. When the group finally comes together, two or three people are selected to share the story about which they most recently made notes.

Summarise your thoughts

Prepare notes for a three-minute speech on:

(a) your favourite hobby

(b) a person who inspires you

(c) your favourite fictional character.

Summarise these notes on a plain note card, using only headings and key words to provide a framework for the structure and prompts for the content.

Place your note card down so you cannot see it, or swap cards with a partner and present a short impromptu speech.

Now, pause

Repeat every sentence below, changing the position of the pause and the word to emphasise every time:

(a) Terry always dresses with flair.

(b) He is unfortunate in his choice of friends.

(c) That is a smart suit.

(d) You look unique.

(e) I am a great performer.

Express your views

This game works best in a large group.

A butcher's shop in a village has closed and has been purchased by a family who wish to open a fast food outlet. Its position would be between a pub and a chemist's shop. There are already two pubs serving food and a restaurant in the village. A public debate will be held in the village hall to decide whether permission should be granted.

Choose a character and enter the debate:

(a) the chairperson of the council

(b) the prospective owner of the fast food outlet

(c) the owner of the pub next door

(d) the owner of the chemist's shop next door

(e) the owner of a flat above the chemist's shop

(f) a local teenager

(g) a local resident.

A similar discussion could be prepared for the following situations:

(a) a company wishes to build a block of flats on the site of an old petrol station

(b) an organisation wishes to turn a former children's home into a halfway house for asylum seekers.

Case studies

This chapter presents case studies of great speeches and speaking techniques. It is suitable for competent speakers and for those wanting to develop exceptional skills for speaking in public.

Good orators rely on most of the key concepts discussed in this book – detailed research, thorough preparation, a clear purpose and a powerful vocal technique. All of these skills can be learned and practised, which will boost your confidence and help you to develop a commanding stage presence.

The speeches were chosen because of their impact or because they demonstrate a valuable concept. By studying the commentary for each speech, you will learn how particular techniques are used in practice.

Each person will have their own approach to a speech and will deliver their messages differently. However, when addressing large groups of people, the words you use must follow recognised rules so all the listeners can understand your message. To this end, standard linguistic devices are used (a shared vocabulary, common grammatical forms, standard syntax and familiar figures of speech) as well as practical devices (pitch, pace, pause, power, inflection and tone).

Now for some examples of speeches! Please bear in mind that the commentary we have provided is a sample of the linguistic devices used within these speeches and is not a definite or conclusive list. You will have your own opinion on what the orator is saying and your own approach to dissecting the speech.

Symbols used in the commentary:

// pause

_ (underline) emphasis

Mark Antony at the Capitol

This speech is taken from the play Julius Caesar *(Act 3, Scene 2) by William Shakespeare. This example, unlike the remaining three examples, is a fictional speech.*

Friends, Romans, countrymen[1], lend me your ears:
I come to bury Caesar, not to praise him.
The evil that men do lives after them:
The good is oft interréd with their bones.
So let it be with Caesar. The noble Brutus
Hath told you Caesar was ambitious[2]:
If it were so[3], it was a grievous fault,
And grievously hath Caesar answered it.
Here, under leave of Brutus and the rest
(For Brutus is an honourable man;
So are they all, all honourable men)[4]
Come I to speak in Caesar's funeral.
He was my friend, faithful and just to me[5];
But Brutus says, he was ambitious,
And Brutus is an honourable[6] man.
He hath brought many captives home to Rome,
Whose ransoms did the general coffers fill.
Did this in Caesar seem ambitious?[7]
When that the poor have cried, Caesar hath wept[8]:
Ambition should be made of sterner stuff.
Yet Brutus says, he was ambitious,
And Brutus is[9] an honourable man.
You all did see, that on the Lupercal
I thrice presented him a kingly crown,
Which he did thrice refuse. Was this ambition?
Yet Brutus says, he was ambitious,
And sure he is an honourable man.

I speak not to disprove what Brutus spoke,
But here I am to speak what I do know[10].
You all did love him once, not without cause:
What cause withholds you then to mourn for him?[11]
O judgement, thou art fled to brutish beasts[12],
And men have lost their reason[13]. Bear with me.
My heart is in the coffin there with Caesar,
And I must pause till it come back to me[14].

Commentary

The main device in this speech is irony. Mark Antony knows
that Brutus and the conspirators and murderers of Caesar are
in control and the only way he is to be allowed to speak is if he
praises them.

1 First of all he identifies himself with the crowd

Friends, // Romans, // countrymen, //

then meets their mood

I come to bury Caesar, // not to praise him.

In this way he has assured himself of his platform with the
people and to some extent with the conspirators, but this must
be strengthened. He is trying to reach an angry, noisy crowd
without shouting. He uses clarity and control of pace, as well
as pause and stress.

2 He continues to identify himself with the crowd by praising
Brutus and the rest and seemingly discrediting Caesar.

3 By using the phrase '*If it were so*' he is casting doubt on the
fact without actually saying so.

4 Pure irony, as he gives Brutus and the other conspirators the
credit for allowing him to speak and praises them.

Here, under leave of Brutus and the rest

(For Brutus is an honourable man; //

So are they all, // all honourable men)

Come I to speak in Caesar's funeral.

Now he has placed himself in a position from which he can, by
stealth, expose Caesar's virtues to the crowd while, with the
strong use of irony, appearing to praise Brutus and the rest.

5 Delivered thoughtfully and sincerely.

6 Emphasis: *And Brutus is an <u>honourable</u> man.*

7 Increase in pace in this sentence, leading up to the rhetorical question, with rising inflection on 'ambitious' and emphasis on 'this'.

He hath brought many captives home to Rome,

Whose ransoms did the general coffers fill.

Did <u>this</u> in Caesar seem ambitious?

8 A synonym – with the stronger (emphasised) word '<u>wept</u>' attributed to Caesar.

9 Emphasis: *And <u>Brutus is</u> an honourable man.*

Now the irony is becoming stronger as Mark Antony is building his case. The delivery of these lines about Brutus becomes more sarcastic, as the tone colour is built. Now he presents them with something that they all witnessed and, therefore, cannot deny:

<u>You all did see</u>, that on the Lupercal

I <u>thrice</u> presented him a kingly crown,

Which he did <u>thrice refuse</u> // [increased stress]

Was <u>this</u> ambition? // [rising inflection, rhetorical question]

Yet Brutus says, he was ambitious,

And <u>sure</u> he is an honourable man.

Tone colour and inflection build the suggestion that what is said is not what is believed.

10 A contrast of two apparently opposing statements, but by using the first he cannot be denied the second. Having given them the facts and reminded them of Caesar's virtues, the next section of the speech is an appeal to their sensibilities.

11 Here the tone softens and the pace slows. *'not without cause'* is emphasised by lowering the voice rather than raising it. Compound inflection (rising, falling, rising) is used on the rhetorical question to express the inherent emotion.

12 'Judgement' is personified as being able to choose where to go and 'brutish beasts' is the metaphor for the conspirators. The whole of this final section is spoken, as though to himself but with the intention of being heard by the crowd.

13 Emotional pause, followed by measured pauses at the end of each line.

Bear with me. //

My heart is in the coffin there with Caesar, //

And I must pause till it come back to me. //

14 He has made his case and now he is using his own emotion for two purposes: to demonstrate to the crowd how they should be feeling, and thereby play on their guilt; and to give them time to consider what he has said.

Throughout the speech the use of irony is predominant – as it is the one way that Mark Antony can be allowed to speak and counter the propaganda that Brutus has fed to the crowd; by reminding them of what Caesar had done and finally what they themselves witnessed and used to feel, he turns the mood around and accomplishes his intentions.

Ursula K. Le Guin

A Left-Handed Commencement Address
(Mills College, Oakland, California, 19 May 1983)

Ursula K. Le Guin (1929–2018) was an American author who wrote mostly fantasy and science fiction. Her works explored anarchist, feminist, psychological and sociological themes.

I want to thank the Mills College Class of '83 for offering me a rare chance: to speak aloud in public in the language of women[1].

I know there are men graduating, and I don't mean to exclude them, far from it. There is a Greek tragedy where the Greek says to the foreigner, 'If you don't understand Greek, please signify by nodding.'[2] Anyhow, commencements are usually operated under the unspoken agreement that everybody graduating is either male[3] or ought to be. That's why we are all wearing these twelfth-century dresses that look so great on men and make women look either like a mushroom or a pregnant stork[4]. Intellectual tradition is male.

Public speaking is done in the public tongue, the national or tribal language; and the language of our tribe is the men's language. Of course women learn it. We're not dumb. If you can tell Margaret Thatcher from Ronald Reagan, or Indira Gandhi from General Somoza, by anything they say, tell me how. This is a man's world, so it talks a man's language. The words are all words of power. You've come a long way, baby, but no way is long enough. You can't even get there by selling yourself out: because there is theirs, not yours.

Maybe we've had enough words of power and talk about the battle of life. Maybe we need some words of weakness. Instead of saying now that I hope you will all go forth from this ivory tower of college into the Real World and forge a triumphant career or at least help your husband to and keep our country strong and be a success in everything – instead of talking about power, what if I talked like a woman right here in public? It won't sound right. It's going to sound terrible. What if I said what I hope for you is first, if – only if – you want kids, I hope you have them. Not hordes of them. A couple, enough[5]. I hope they're beautiful. I hope you and they have enough to eat, and a place to be warm and clean in, and friends, and work you like doing. Well, is that what you went to college for? Is that all? What about success?[6]

Success is somebody else's failure. Success is the American Dream we can keep dreaming because most people in most places, including thirty million of ourselves, live wide awake in the terrible reality of poverty. No, I do not wish you success. I don't even want to talk about it. I want to talk about failure.

Because you are human beings you are going to meet failure. You are going to meet disappointment, injustice, betrayal, and irreparable loss. You will find you're weak where you thought yourself strong. You'll work for possessions and then find they possess you. You will find yourself – as I know you already have – in dark places, alone, and afraid[7].

What I hope for you, for all my sisters and daughters, brothers and sons, is that you will be able to live there, in the dark place. To live in the place that our rationalizing culture of success denies, calling it a place of exile, uninhabitable, foreign.

Well, we're already foreigners. Women as women are largely excluded from, alien to, the self-declared male norms of this society, where human beings are called Man[8], the only respectable god is male, the only direction is up[9]. So that's their country; let's explore our own. I'm not talking about sex; that's a whole other universe, where every man and woman is on their own. I'm talking about society, the so-called man's world of institutionalized competition, aggression, violence, authority, and power. If we want to live as women, some separatism is forced upon us: Mills College is a wise embodiment of that separatism. The war-games world wasn't made by us or for us; we can't even breathe the air there without masks. And if you put the mask on you'll have a hard time getting it off[10]. So how about going on doing things our own way, as to some extent you did here at Mills? Not for men and the male power hierarchy – that's their game. Not against men, either – that's still playing by their rules. But with any men who are with us: that's our game. Why should a free woman with a college education either fight Macho-man or serve him? Why should she live her life on his terms?

Macho-man is afraid of our terms, which are not all rational, positive, competitive, etc. And so he has taught us to despise and deny them. In our society, women have lived, and have been despised for living, the whole side of life that includes and takes responsibility for helplessness, weakness, and illness, for the irrational and the irreparable, for all that is obscure, passive, uncontrolled, animal, unclean – the valley of the shadow, the deep, the depths of life. All that the Warrior denies and refuses is left to us and the men who share it with us and therefore, like us, can't play doctor, only nurse, can't be warriors, only civilians, can't be chiefs, only indians[11]. Well, so that is our country. The night side of our country. If there is a day side to it, high sierras, prairies of bright grass, we only know pioneers' tales about it, we haven't got there yet. We're never going to get there by imitating Macho-man. We are only going to get there by going our own way, by living there, by living through the night in our own country.

So what I hope for you is that you live there not as prisoners, ashamed of being women, consenting captives of a psychopathic social system[12], but as natives[13]. That you will be at home there, keep house there, be your own mistress, with a room of your own. That you will do your work there, whatever you're good at, art or science or tech or running a company or sweeping under the beds, and when they tell you that it's second-class work because a woman is doing it, I hope you tell them to go to hell and while they're going to give you equal pay for equal time. I hope you live without the need to dominate, and without the need to be dominated. I hope you are never victims, but I hope you have no power over other people. And when you fail, and are defeated, and in pain, and in the dark, then I hope you will remember that darkness is your country, where you live, where no wars are fought and no wars are won, but where the future is. Our roots are in the dark; the earth is our country[14]. Why did we look up for blessing – instead of around, and down? What hope we have lies there. Not in the sky full of orbiting spy-eyes and weaponry, but in the earth we have looked down upon. Not from above, but from below. Not in the light that blinds, but in the dark that nourishes, where human beings grow human souls[15].

Commentary

This speech contains allegory, metaphor, anecdote, sarcasm, irony and rhetorical questions. It is an argument from a feminist perspective about semantics, the use of language and the encoding of messages. The theme concerns the masculinisation of language in its efforts to encourage graduates to strive for empowerment, success and the total denial of disappointment, injustice, betrayal and any form of weakness.

1 She sets out her intentions and arrests the attention of her audience in the opening challenge, when she thanks them for the opportunity of speaking in public *'in the language of women'*. We are drawn in by two unspoken questions: is it rare for women to speak aloud in public? And what is the *'language of women'*?

2 She uses sarcasm, by pretending to acknowledge the male graduates, but the anecdote from Greek theatre implies an allegory: 'If you do not understand what I am saying because you are male, please signify by nodding'. In other words, she is about to speak to women in a language the men will not understand anyway.

3 A dramatic pause, as she begins her strong challenge to the status quo and uses sarcasm (*all graduates are men*) leading to her climax: // *Intellectual tradition is male* //

4 Humour through ridiculous similes… *make women look either like a mushroom* // *or a pregnant stork*. This engages the audience early in the speech.

5 Even though this is a formal event (and they are all wearing dresses that make them look like mushrooms) she uses informal language here (*it's,* not *it is; kids,* not *children; hordes,* not *many*) to create an intimate tone, which draws her audience into a conspiracy, the secret 'other world' she is inviting them to join.

6 Three rhetorical questions with rising inflection to the climax: *What about success?* //

7 Grouping in threes is a common and effective pattern. There are three sentences based on 'you will find', ended by a list of three: *in dark places, alone, and afraid.*

8 Irony: to call humankind 'Man' is to ignore half the population.

9 Another hyperbole. Nobody believes *the only direction is up.* We know what she is trying to say but this continued exaggeration of the state of affairs might weaken the effectiveness of her argument.

10 The mask is a metaphor for the 'mask' women wear when pretending to be men, speaking as men, thinking as men. The metaphor is an effective and memorable image because it is relevant to the situation and echoes the theme of male aggression, violence and war.

11 Her argument throughout the piece is that the rules of life are invented and imposed by a patriarchal society and even society itself is a masculine institution. The paragraph is full of contrasts and metaphors as she paints the picture of macho man versus nurturing women, demonstrated in her comparisons and contrasts in metaphor, of always being nurses not doctors, civilians not warriors.

12 The alliteration in *consenting captives of a psychopathic social system* and the hyperbole (women are not really being murdered by the masculine bias) strengthen her repeated criticism of how wrong the system is.

13 The final paragraph is addressed completely to women. It summarises what she has been addressing throughout the speech and finalises the argument with a repeat of the first four lines she used in the beginning of the second main paragraph.

14 She has built the metaphor of the collected matriarchal values being a country, and now equates this 'country' with the earth, making it a more powerful metaphor because the earth is present beneath every member of the audience, and they are thus automatically part of her 'country'. This demonstrates how metaphors can be used to involve an audience. She first linked her point of view with a metaphor, reinforced the metaphor, then reassigned the metaphor to something of undeniable

SPEAKING MATTERS

value, and the audience is thus subtly led to believe that her point of view is true. If she had simply stated 'women support all life and so are as important as the earth' her audience would not have understood her. The metaphorical language helps to support her argument by the association of ideas.

15 Her concluding reference to *human beings* and *human souls* is highly inclusive, uniting the audience members and establishing common ground.

CASE STUDIES

Queen Elizabeth I

The Spanish Armada speech (1588)

Queen Elizabeth I (1533–1603) was Queen of England and Ireland from 1558 until her death in 1603. This speech was addressed to the English army at Tilbury Fort in 1588, when invasion by the Spanish Armada was imminent. A force of 4,000 soldiers was stationed there to defend the capital city against any incursion upriver. She went to address them personally to rally and inspire them. The defeat of the Armada associated her with one of the greatest victories in English history.

(The speech is reported by Dr Sharp. The spelling has been modernised. Despite the possibility that Sharp may have embellished the language and structure, it is a great example of a rousing, patriotic speech.)

My loving people[1], we have been persuaded by some, that are careful of our safety, to take heed how we commit ourselves to armed multitudes, for fear of treachery; but I assure you, I do not desire to live to distrust my faithful and loving people.

Let tyrants fear; I have always so behaved myself that, under God, I have placed my chiefest strength and safeguard in the loyal hearts and good will of my subjects[2]. And therefore I am come amongst you at this time, not as for my recreation or sport, but being resolved, in the midst and heat of the battle, to live or die amongst you all; to lay down, for my God, and for my kingdom, and for my people, my honour and my blood, even in the dust[3].

I know I have but the body of a weak and feeble woman[4]; but I have the heart of a king, and of a king of England, too; and think foul scorn that Parma or Spain, or any prince[5] of Europe, should dare to invade the borders of my realms: to which, rather than any dishonour should grow by me, I myself will take up arms; I myself will be your general, judge, and rewarder[6] of every one of your virtues in the field.

115

I know already, by your forwardness, that you have deserved rewards and crowns; and we do assure you, on the word of a prince, that shall be duly paid you. In the meantime my lieutenant general shall be in my stead[7], than whom never prince commanded a more noble and worthy subject; not doubting by your obedience to my general[8], by your concord in the camp, and by your valour in the field, we[9] shall shortly have a famous victory over the enemies of my[10] God, of my kingdom, and of my people[11].

Commentary

Queen Elizabeth I was a great politician and stateswoman and would have understood the dangers that the Spanish fleet imposed upon the shores of England. In the defeat of the Armada, Elizabeth depended largely on the reliability of her sea captains; but she recognised that the soldiers stationed at Tilbury might be needed, as they would defend the capital if Spanish ships came upriver. The delivery of this speech would have been controlled, confident and clear. It needed good modulation and a passionate tone.

1   She begins with a term of endearment and affection and continues this throughout the first lines. Every comma is an opportunity for a pause. She compels their trust by declaring that she has been warned of treachery, but she trusts them despite the danger. This is appropriate to her audience – soldiers respect boldness.

2   The Tudor dynasty was considered mostly tyrannical. Elizabeth, however, ignores this and presents herself as a monarch who loves and cares for her people. Here again she appeals to their affection and emotions before building to a passionate declaration.

3   She is willing to die among them if necessary, for England's sake. After such a declaration by a woman, no man would dream of backing down in the heat of the battle. It was a clever ploy.

4   In keeping with the attitude of the times and her entirely male audience. They might have been struggling with the concept of being told what to do by a mere woman, so she panders to them by acknowledging her vulnerability, then cleverly follows it with the steel and determination in her veins from her inheritance (calling on a respected authority figure, the King of England) and establishes common ground with her audience by declaring what every soldier must feel about the invaders.

5   To intensify her scorn for the invaders she refers to them as princes of Europe (to contrast with Queen and King) and shows how brave she is by vowing to take up arms.

6   Having appealed to their affections, then to their manly pride, then their national pride, she now appeals to their pockets and their purses and suggests rewards. This promise of rewards is continued and increased in the final paragraph.

7   Having claimed the respect from the men for her promise to take up arms, she deftly appoints her lieutenant general in her stead, which is just subterfuge, but it is done so smoothly that it is hard to notice.

8   Instead of pleading with them from a position of weakness she *compels* them by declaring that she does not doubt their obedience. This places the soldiers in the weaker position, because they do not want to fail someone who has publicly declared her faith in them.

9   In '*we* [not you] *shall shortly have a* <u>*famous*</u> *victory*' she reinforces her implication that she will be part of the fighting, but makes no promise of sharing the power (*my God, my kingdom, my people*), leaving an impression of a strong monarch and reinforcing the idea that they are fighting for her, not for freedom.

10 England was under threat of invasion by an army that championed the Roman Catholic religion and thus 'my' God is also a reference to the Protestant faith that Queen Elizabeth represented.

11 Repetition (three), creating a powerful conclusion to stamp her authority on their minds.

This is a rousing speech worthy of a great queen at such a moment of danger. It offers reassurance in the ability of the monarchy to lead a successful campaign, and suggests that victory will be God-given and certain. She inspires love, loyalty and valour and projects a powerful air of unity and defiance against the potential invaders.

Barack Obama

Inaugural Address (20 January 2009)

Presented by Barack Hussein Obama as he became the 44th President of the United States of America.

My fellow citizens,

I stand here today humbled by the task before us, grateful for the trust you have bestowed, mindful of the sacrifices borne by our ancestors. I thank President Bush for his service to our nation, as well as the generosity and co-operation he has shown throughout[2] this transition.

Forty-four Americans have now taken the presidential oath. The words have been spoken during rising tides[1] of prosperity and the still waters of peace. Yet, every so often the oath is taken amidst gathering clouds and raging storms. At these moments, America has carried on not simply because of the skill or vision of those in high office, but because we, the people, have remained faithful to the ideals of our forebears, and true to our founding documents. So it has been. So it must be with this generation of Americans.

That we are in the midst of crisis is now well understood. Our nation is at war, against a far-reaching network of violence and hatred. Our economy is badly weakened, a consequence of greed and irresponsibility on the part of some, but also our collective failure to make hard choices and prepare the nation for a new age. Homes have been lost; jobs shed; businesses shuttered. Our health care is too costly; our schools fail too many; and each day brings further evidence that the ways we use energy strengthen our adversaries and threaten our planet. These are the indicators of crisis, subject to data and statistics. Less measurable but no less profound is a sapping of confidence across our land – a nagging fear that America's decline is inevitable, and that the next generation must lower its sights.

Today I say to you that the challenges we face are real. They are serious and they are many. They will not be met easily or in a short span of time. But know this, America – they will be met.

On this day, we gather because we have chosen hope over fear, unity of purpose over conflict and discord.

On this day, we come to proclaim an end to the petty grievances and false promises, the recriminations and worn out dogmas, that for far too long have strangled our politics.

We remain a young nation, but in the words of Scripture, the time has come to set aside childish things. The time has come to reaffirm our enduring spirit; to choose our better history; to carry forward that precious gift, that noble idea, passed on from generation to generation: the God-given promise that all are equal, all are free, and all deserve a chance to pursue their full measure of happiness.

In reaffirming the greatness of our nation, we understand that greatness is never a given. It must be earned. Our journey has never been one of shortcuts or settling for less. It has not been the path for the faint-hearted – for those who prefer leisure over work, or seek only the pleasures of riches and fame. Rather, it has been the risk-takers, the doers, the makers of things – some celebrated but more often men and women obscure in their labour, who have carried us up the long, rugged path towards prosperity and freedom.

For us, they packed up their few worldly possessions and travelled across oceans in search of a new life. For us, they toiled in sweatshops and settled the West; endured the lash of the whip and ploughed the hard earth. For us, they fought and died, in places like Concord and Gettysburg; Normandy and Khe Sahn.

Time and again these men and women struggled and sacrificed and worked till their hands were raw so that we might live a better life. They saw America as bigger than the sum of our individual ambitions; greater than all the differences of birth or wealth or faction.

This is the journey we continue today. We remain the most prosperous, powerful nation on earth. Our workers are no less productive than when this crisis began. Our minds are no less inventive, our goods and services no less needed than they were last week or last month or last year. Our capacity remains undiminished. But our time of standing pat, of protecting narrow interests and putting off unpleasant decisions – that time has surely passed. Starting today, we must pick ourselves up, dust ourselves off, and begin again the work of remaking America. For everywhere we look, there is work to be done. The state of the economy calls for action, bold and swift and we will act – not only to create new jobs, but to lay a new foundation for growth. We will build the roads and bridges, the electric grids and digital lines that feed our commerce and bind us together. We will restore science to its rightful place, and wield technology's wonders to raise health care's quality and lower its cost. We will harness the sun and the winds and the soil to fuel our cars and run our factories. And we will transform our schools and colleges and universities to meet the demands of a new age. All this we can do. All this we will do.

Now, there are some who question the scale of our ambitions – who suggest that our system cannot tolerate too many big plans. Their memories are short. For they have forgotten what this country has already done; what free men and women can achieve when imagination is joined to common purpose, and necessity to courage. What the cynics fail to understand is that the ground has shifted beneath them – that the stale political arguments that have consumed us for so long no longer apply. The question we ask today is not whether our government is too big or too small, but whether it works – whether it helps families find jobs at a decent wage, care they can afford, a retirement that is dignified. Where the answer is yes, we intend to move forward. Where the answer is no, programs will end. And those of us who manage the public's dollars will be held to account – to spend wisely, reform bad habits, and do our business in the light of day – because only then can we restore the vital trust between a people and their government.

Nor is the question before us whether the market is a force for good or ill. Its power to generate wealth and expand freedom is unmatched, but this crisis has reminded us that without a watchful eye, the market can spin out of control – that a nation cannot prosper long when it favours only the prosperous. The success of our economy has always depended not just on the size of our gross domestic product, but on the reach of our prosperity; on the ability to extend opportunity to every willing heart – not out of charity, but because it is the surest route to our common good.

As for our common defence, we reject as false the choice between our safety and our ideals. Our founding fathers, faced with perils we can scarcely imagine, drafted a charter to assure the rule of law and the rights of man, a charter expanded by the blood of generations. Those ideals still light the world, and we will not give them up for expedience's sake. And so to all other peoples and governments who are watching today, from the grandest capitals to the small village where my father was born: know that America is a friend of each nation and every man, woman and child who seeks a future of peace and dignity, and we are ready to lead once more. Recall that earlier generations faced down fascism and communism not just with missiles and tanks, but with the sturdy alliances and enduring convictions. They understood that our power alone cannot protect us, nor does it entitle us to do as we please. Instead, they knew that our power grows through its prudent use; our security emanates from the justness of our cause, the force of our example, the tempering qualities of humility and restraint.

We are the keepers of this legacy. Guided by these principles once more, we can meet those new threats that demand even greater effort – even greater cooperation and understanding between nations. We will begin to responsibly leave Iraq to its people, and forge a hard-earned peace in Afghanistan. With old friends and former foes, we will work tirelessly to lessen the nuclear threat, and roll back the spectre of a warming planet. We will not apologize for our way of life, nor will we waver in its defence, and for those who seek to advance their aims by inducing terror and slaughtering innocents[3], we say to you now that our spirit is stronger and cannot be broken; you cannot outlast us, and we will defeat you.

For we know that our patchwork heritage is a strength, not a weakness. We are a nation of Christians and Muslims, Jews and Hindus – and non-believers. We are shaped by every language and culture, drawn from every end of this earth; and because we have tasted the bitter swill of civil war and segregation, and emerged from that dark chapter stronger and more united, we cannot help but believe that the old hatreds shall someday pass; that the lines of tribe shall soon dissolve; that as the world grows smaller, our common humanity shall reveal itself; and that America must play its role in ushering in a new era of peace. To the Muslim world, we seek a new way forward, based on mutual interest and mutual respect. To those leaders around the globe who seek to sow conflict, or blame their society's ills on the West[4] – know that your people will judge you on what you can build, not what you destroy. To those who cling to power through corruption and deceit and the silencing of dissent, know that you are on the wrong side of history; but that we will extend a hand if you are willing to unclench your fist. To the people of poor nations, we pledge to work alongside you to make your farms flourish and let clean waters flow; to nourish starved bodies and feed hungry minds. And to those nations like ours that enjoy relative plenty, we say we can no longer afford indifference to suffering outside our borders; nor can we consume the world's resources without regard to effect. For the world has changed, and we must change with it.

As we consider the road that unfolds before us, we remember with humble gratitude those brave Americans who, at this very hour, patrol far-off deserts and distant mountains. They have something to tell us, just as the fallen heroes who lie in Arlington whisper through the ages. We honour them not only because they are guardians of our liberty, but because they embody the spirit of service; a willingness to find meaning in something greater than themselves. And yet, at this moment – a moment that will define a generation – it is precisely this spirit that must inhabit us all.

For as much as government can do and must do, it is ultimately the faith and determination of the American people upon which this nation relies[5]. It is the kindness to take in a stranger when the levees break, the selflessness of workers who would rather cut their hours than see a friend lose their job which sees us through our darkest hours. It is the firefighter's courage to storm a stairway filled with smoke, but also a parent's willingness to nurture a child, that finally decides our fate.

Our challenges may be new. The instruments with which we meet them may be new. But those values upon which our success depends – honesty and hard work, courage and fair play, tolerance and curiosity, loyalty and patriotism – these things are old. These things are true. They have been the quiet force of progress throughout our history. What is demanded then is a return to these truths. What is required of us now is a new era of responsibility – a recognition, on the part of every American, that we have duties to ourselves, our nation, and the world, duties that we do not grudgingly accept but rather seize gladly, firm in the knowledge that there is nothing so satisfying to the spirit, so defining of our character, than giving our all to a difficult task. This is the price and the promise of citizenship. This is the source of our confidence – the knowledge that God calls on us to shape an uncertain destiny. This is the meaning of our liberty and our creed – why men and women and children of every race and every faith can join in celebration across this magnificent mall, and why a man whose father less than 60 years ago might not have been served at a local restaurant can now stand before you to take a most sacred oath. So let us mark this day with remembrance, of who we are and how far we have travelled. In the year of America's birth, in the coldest of months, a small band of patriots huddled by dying campfires on the shores of an icy river. The capital was abandoned. The enemy was advancing. The snow was stained with blood. At a moment when the outcome of our revolution was most in doubt, the father of our nation ordered these words be read to the people:

'Let it be told to the future world…that in the depth of winter, when nothing but hope and virtue could survive…that the city and the country, alarmed at one common danger, came forth to meet [it][6].'

America. In the face of our common dangers, in this winter of our hardship, let us remember these timeless words. With hope and virtue, let us brave once more the icy currents, and endure what storms may come. Let it be said by our children's children that when we were tested we refused to let this journey end, that we did not turn back nor did we falter; and with eyes fixed on the horizon and God's grace upon us, we carried forth that great gift of freedom and delivered it safely to future generations. Thank you. God bless you. And God bless the United States of America.

Commentary

Read the speech carefully, noting the allusions, references and metaphors. Note similarities with his victory speech and with the inaugural speech of John F Kennedy.

An inaugural speech is intended to introduce the incoming president to those who voted for him, to the rest of the country, and to lay out his attitudes toward and plans for the next few years. He should try to be all things to all men, bring everyone on board, be firm and fair in leadership and convey all this in noble rhetorical language and within a forward-looking yet historical context. How far does Obama's speech meet these aims?

1 The rhetoric of the metaphors *'rising tides of prosperity', 'still waters of peace', 'gathering clouds and raging storms'* are obvious descriptions of the current economic climate and precede the concluding quotation from George Washington: 'brave once more the icy currents, and endure what storms may come'. This grand language raises the significance of the speech and the quotation from Thomas Paine (along with his references elsewhere to Abraham Lincoln and here to Concord and Gettysburg) evokes the proud history of the nation.

125

2 The positive side is conveyed in 'skill' and 'vision', 'faithful to ideals', 'the greatness of our nation'. His use of pronouns is significant and carefully chosen. He uses the first person singular twice in the first two sentences – and thereafter only once – 'I say to you'. He uses the second person to apply almost exclusively to enemies and to other nations. His personal approach is inclusive to Americans so he uses 'we' and 'us' extensively to suggest a common heritage and working together.

3 References to God and biblical language (*'slaughtering innocents'*) and use of formal language (*'nation', 'liberty', 'the road that unfolds before us'*) enhance the message, while the mixed metaphor of the *'dark chapter'* of the *'bitter swill of civil war and segregation'* powerfully expresses the worst side of America's history.

4 Throughout the speech, which is more serious and less emotionally popularist than his famous 'yes we can' acceptance speech, the nation's problems of war, terrorism, climate change and the economy are alluded to obliquely (*'this crisis', 'lessen the nuclear threat, and roll back the spectre of a warming planet'*, those *'who seek to sow conflict, or blame their society's ills on the West'*) and linked to the USA's strength and willingness to overcome adversity. Freedom is a *'long rugged path'*, the *'fallen heroes who lie in Arlington'* military cemetery are evoked and *'we will extend a hand if you are willing to unclench your fist'*. This is a combination of strength without aggression. The criticism of violent ways: *'Your people will judge you on what you can build, not what you destroy'* is precisely and powerfully expressed.

5 He emphasises the notion of responsibility – by politicians and by citizens, by the doers and the makers; those who toiled, endured, fought and died; and those who will build, restore, harness and transform. *'For as much as government can do and must do, it is ultimately the faith and determination of the American people upon which this nation relies.'*

6 His final extract, taken directly from Thomas Paine (*The Crisis*, 1776), draws parallels between the brave struggles of America as a nation (fighting the British for independence) and the present day when the US is simultaneously fighting wars and an economic crisis. Evoking the triumphs and bravery of American forebears and heroes strengthens his case to remember the past and carry on to the future.

This was a powerful and resonant speech. Its strength lies in its expression of intent, laying out of plans and signalling of changes in attitude, rather than squeezing out emotions through empty rhetoric.

There are memorable phrases:

'We will extend a hand if you are willing to unclench your fist'

'Your people will judge you on what you can build, not what you destroy'

'As for our common defence, we reject as false the choice between our safety and our ideals'.

It is well crafted (Jon Favreau is his speechwriter) and noble (Obama has a relaxed yet commanding voice and demeanour). He makes eye contact with his audience and uses pausing to highlight key words in an effective way. It is this mixture and balance between the powerful content of his speech and the way in which it is delivered which makes its impact so strong and persuasive.

Acknowledgements

William Shakespeare: *Mark Antony at the Capitol* as found in
Julius Caesar (Act 3, Scene 2).
The version used in this publication is, as set out, in: Proudfoot,
R., Thompson, A. and Kastan D. S. (ed.) (2015) *Shakespeare
Complete Works*, Revised Edition, India: The Arden Shakespeare,
an imprint of Bloomsbury Publishing PLC.

Ursula K. Le Guin: *A Left-Handed Commencement Address*
(Mills College, Oakland, California, 19 May 1983).
This address is not under copyright, and may be quoted or
reprinted as a whole without obtaining permission.

Queen Elizabeth I: *The Spanish Armada speech (1588)*.
This speech is not under copyright, and may be quoted or
reprinted as a whole without obtaining permission.

Barack Obama: *Inaugural Address (20 January 2009)*.
Pursuant to federal law, government-produced materials
appearing on the White House website are not copyright
protected.